THE *Dragon* FAMILY

(Lochguard Highland Dragons #5)

Jessie Donovan

This book is a work of fiction. Names, characters, places, and incidents are either the product of the writer's imagination or are used fictitiously, and any resemblance to actual persons, living or dead, business establishments, events, or locales is entirely coincidental.

The Dragon Family

Mythical Lake Press, LLC
First Print Edition

Cover Art by Clarissa Yeo of Yocla Designs
ISBN: 978-1942211624

Other Books by Jessie Donovan

Stonefire Dragons

Sacrificed to the Dragon
Seducing the Dragon
Revealing the Dragons
Healed by the Dragon
Reawakening the Dragon
Loved by the Dragon
Surrendering to the Dragon
Cured by the Dragon
Aiding the Dragon
Finding the Dragon
Craved by the Dragon
Persuading the Dragon (2019)

Lochguard Highland Dragons

The Dragon's Dilemma
The Dragon Guardian
The Dragon's Heart
The Dragon Warrior
The Dragon Family

Kelderan Runic Warriors

The Conquest
The Barren
The Heir
The Forbidden (Aug 2018)

Asylums for Magical Threats

Blaze of Secrets
Frozen Desires
Shadow of Temptation
Flare of Promise

Cascade Shifters

Convincing the Cougar
Reclaiming the Wolf
Cougar's First Christmas
Resisting the Cougar

Chapter One

Finlay Stewart stared at the folders in his email account and tried to ignore the number of messages in the "Family-related Complaints" folder.

Fifty-one.

Fifty-one messages in the last week from clan members voicing a concern or complaint related to his three cousins: Faye, Fraser, and Fergus MacKenzie. Their recent behavior only highlighted how much of a taming influence their mother—his Aunt Lorna—had over her brood.

Aunt Lorna had been gone just over a week, taking a much-delayed honeymoon with her human mate, Ross. Chaos had erupted shortly thereafter.

His dragon grunted. *It's not chaos. Just a few incidents, which you should expect from our cousins. If we weren't clan leader, you would probably be up to a few things, too.*

But I am clan leader. That means I need to sort things out.

A quick call from Aunt Lorna would put everything back to rights.

Since he wasn't about to call his aunt and ask her to cut her holiday short, he ignored his beast and focused back on the emails. Clicking the latest one related to Faye, from Sylvia MacAllister, he read:

Faye's most recent argument in my restaurant went beyond social acceptance. She yelled, tossed a plate at her mate, and eventually stormed out. I understand she's pregnant, and she's also my daughter's friend, but if she keeps this up, I won't have any customers at all.

Faye was his youngest cousin and had always been the most temperamental of his kin. However, in recent weeks, her pregnancy had turned her explosive whenever she was around her mate, Grant.

And considering Sylvia was the mother to the five MacAllister siblings and daughter of the notorious troublemaker Archie, Faye's display in the restaurant must've been something indeed to merit a complaint.

His dragon spoke up. *Talk to Faye's mate. He's the only one who can keep her in line.*

He's been busy. Besides, she should listen to me. I'm family and clan leader.

Right, because Faye has always listened to us in the past just because we said she had to.

Not dignifying his dragon with a response, Finn moved on to an email with the subject line: Fergus MacKenzie lost another contact. He read it:

Fergus didn't show up for work today and missed an important call with one of our clan's contacts. A Protector mentioned seeing him fly off into the sunrise this morning. I don't know what's going on, but this is the third time this week he's flown off without a word. If he keeps it up, I will have to replace him.

Fergus worked as an intelligence analyst for Clan Lochguard. Usually, he was a model employee, always the first to arrive, and completed the work of two males in the same amount of time it took one average employee to do the same.

However, Fergus had been fighting off a mate-claim

frenzy for months, allowing his human mate, Gina, to rest after the birth of her son.

His dragon huffed. *Why doesn't he listen to Gina? She says she's ready as soon as someone is able to watch wee Jamie for the duration of the frenzy. Aunt Lorna has offered several times.*

Fergus has always believed he knows better, especially when it comes to protecting those he loves. His mating is still new, and with a baby since the beginning, they probably haven't had as much time to get to know each other as we and Ara did.

Arabella MacLeod was Finn's mate, and mother to their young triplets.

His beast grunted. *Then talk with him. You're the only one Fergus listens to about such matters, apart from Aunt Lorna.*

I've tried, as has Fraser. I think I need to discuss this situation with Ara. She always has new suggestions on how to handle my cousins.

At the mention of Arabella, Finn paused and listened for the smallest sound of an infant fussing. However, the silence meant that the triplets and his mate were still asleep, so he needed to do as much work as he could while he had the chance.

If there was one thing being a new father had taught him, it was that he'd wasted a lot of time in the past. But no longer. The more he wasted, the less time he would spend with his mate and children.

Since his current task was to find a way to rein in his cousins, he clicked one more email related to his last cousin Fraser. It was from the clan's head doctor, Dr. Layla MacFie:

Fraser spends every moment he can shadowing Holly. Holly was Fraser's human mate. *I understand that she's eight months pregnant with twins, but I check her health daily and continue to monitor all three of them. Holly is healthy and merely waiting for their bairns to be born. And as we're still trying to find more staff for the surgery, I need Holly's help more than ever. Is there nothing else that Fraser should be doing? I need him out of my surgery.*

With a sigh, Finn leaned back in his chair. Fraser's recent big project, to design and oversee the construction of a large clan warehouse, had been completed in recent weeks. Finn assumed that there were other people waiting in line for one of Fraser's designs since he had a unique and in-demand approach. So why the bloody hell was he wasting what time he had before the birth of his children following Holly around?

His dragon said in an almost bored tone, *You know about Holly's miscarriage with their first child. He's nervous.*

But the bairns are nearly to term. Bloody hell, Holly's had more monitoring and health checks than Arabella ever did, and she carried three children.

Still, the loss stays with them both. Maybe inviting everyone to dinner would be best, after talking with Ara about what to do. That way, we can address this all at once. And if we lock the doors, it'll make it difficult for them to leave.

Aye, and that also makes it hard for us to escape.

He heard the first stirrings of one of his children via the baby monitor. Standing, Finn spoke to his dragon again as he walked, *Arabella does function better on little sleep and will probably have an idea other than smacking each one on the back of the head. Although, Ara would do that in a heartbeat if it came to it.*

His beast snorted. *So instead of Aunt Lorna, you're going to allow your mate to sort out your family?*

We'll do it together. The MacKenzie siblings are like my

brothers and sister, and the oldest telling the others what to do usually doesn't work.

Finn entered one of two nurseries they used for the children. To help Arabella and still do his clan leader duties, they often put the lads in one room and Freya in another during the day. That way, his mate wasn't stuck with all three children.

He and Arabella also switched duties with the best-behaved baby—their daughter—and the identical twin boys. Today was Finn's turn with Freya.

His only daughter lay in her crib, making little noises and waving her arms. Finn swooped her up and cuddled her against his chest. After kissing her blonde head, he murmured, "Just like Mummy, aren't you? Wide-eyed and awake with the least amount of sleep."

Freya merely slapped her hand against his chest.

With a chuckle, he moved Freya to the changing table. Despite the squirming and her attempts to jump off the table, Finn managed to change her nappy. When he finished, he raised her top and blew against her stomach. Freya squealed, and so he did it again.

Arabella's voice came from behind him. "No wonder it takes you so long to get her up."

Glancing over his shoulder, he saw Arabella smiling, one son in each arm. "Aye, well, I don't have to rush and worry about one of the wee lads pissing on me during the nappy changing."

"If I remember correctly, you laughed the first time it happened to me."

Picking up Freya, he moved to his mate's side and wrapped his free arm around her and his sons. "It was funny then. Now, however, I swear the lads use me as target practice more often than not."

Arabella snorted. "They take after their father, from

what I hear."

Leaning down, he kissed his mate gently. "And you wouldn't have it any other way."

As he stared into his mate's brown eyes and held his family close, a part of Finn wished he could whisk them away for a holiday on the Isle of Skye, where Lochguard had some protected training grounds that occasionally doubled as holiday cottages. He'd love nothing more than a week with his family, absolved of any responsibility.

However, until the threat of dragon hunters and Dragon Knights were banished, he couldn't risk leaving Lochguard unprotected.

The son whom they thought took the most after him personality-wise, Declan, squealed right into Finn's ear. He moved his gaze to the lad with dark hair and eyes like Arabella's and winked. "I know everyone wants my full attention, but let's try to avoid making me deaf this early, aye?"

Arabella shook her head. "He's only a few months old. I'm sure he doesn't understand the concept of deafness."

"Ah, but all my children will be clever and braw, so I see no need to treat them any less."

She raised an eyebrow. "Should we put that to the test? I can easily go out for the day and allow you to take care of all three of them. With your supposed baby-whispering skills, it should be a walk in the park."

"I could manage."

Arabella snorted. "Bloody stubborn dragonman." She readjusted her hold on their other son, Grayson. "But enough of that. I can tell something's on your mind, Finn. What is it?"

Freya put her fist into her mouth and chewed on her knuckles with her toothless gums. "As you feed the children, I'll explain it to you."

He motioned toward the living area and they made their

way. Arabella placed one son and then the other in their bouncy baby seats, fastening the belts of each in turn.

Grayson immediately frowned. She bopped each nose in turn. "Now, now, I know you love Mummy best, but give Daddy a chance."

Finn handed off Freya to her mother. "They only like you best because you're the food source."

Arabella settled on the couch, raised up her top and undid her nursing bra. As soon as Freya latched on, she raised her brows at Finn. "My breasts are never going to be the same again. I sure hope they like me best."

He moved to trace Arabella's cheek, but Grayson chose that moment to start crying.

Undoing the belt and scooping up his son, he gently rocked him and murmured, "Now, now, Gray. I know you're hungry, but I need to tell Mummy she's beautiful." Glancing up at Arabella, he took in the sight of his daughter and mate. "Both of my lasses are beautiful."

A blush crept up Arabella's neck. "Finn."

"It's true." Gray's cries died down and he kissed his son's forehead. "And one day you'll help me protect them, Gray."

His son reached for Finn's face and dug his sharp, little bairn nails into his skin. Finn leaned back a fraction. "I know you're just showing me you're ready to protect the family, but try not to hurt your dad, aye?"

He heard Arabella whisper, "You'll help protect the family as well, Freya. As much as dragon males like to think they should be the only ones ensuring our safety, we protect those we love, too. Your Auntie Faye will give you lessons from an early age, I'm sure."

Holding Gray close, Finn bounced in place and met Arabella's gaze again. "Speaking of Faye, Aunt Lorna leaving has caused more of a problem than I'd anticipated." He explained the situations around each of his cousins before continuing, “Do you have any ideas beyond scolding them?”

“You deal with these types of things every day. Why is it so hard with your family? If Tristan were acting like an arsehole, I’d tell him.”

Tristan was Arabella’s older brother, who lived on Clan Stonefire in Northern England. While not the friendliest of brothers-in-law, there was much Finn admired about the dragonman. “Aye, well, your brother is a special type of male. I think anyone would tell him that.”

She raised an eyebrow. “Let’s add that to the list of things I need to tell him the next time I speak to him.”

He sighed. “Ara...”

“Okay, okay. If it weren’t Faye, Fraser, and Fergus, what would you do?”

He didn’t hesitate. “Invite each to my office and discuss their problems.”

She nodded. “Exactly. So, why not do that?”

“Because they’re Faye, Fraser, and Fergus. I’m merely their cousin. Aye, they’ll listen when it’s an emergency situation, but I’m not sure this classifies.”

“If the clan starts to doubt your leadership abilities, it does.”

Leave it to Arabella to lay out the truth without any sugarcoating.

It was one of the many reasons he loved her.

Declan wiggled in his bouncy seat on the floor, and despite the belt around his middle, he came close to rolling off the side. Finn quickly placed Grayson into the playpen and scooped up his other son. “Learn to walk, Dec, and you won’t have to lay down in those blasted things.”

Declan merely blew a giant spit bubble.

As he scrunched his eyes and made a funny face, Finn said, “See? Family doesn’t find me intimidating.” Arabella merely tilted her head and he added, “I can be intimidating.

Scary, even."

Arabella burst out laughing and continued to do it for a full minute. Freya even stopped eating in the process and started wailing.

Getting a hold of herself, Arabella murmured apologies to Freya. As soon as their daughter was eating again, Arabella said, "Being scary isn't your way, Finn, and you know it. You're good at roping in others to help you, but not through intimidation."

"Maybe," he grumbled.

She glanced down at Freya, who had finished eating. As she propped their daughter into a sitting position on her leg and gently patted her back, she said, "Daddy doesn't understand how charming he is. I may not admit it often, but it's one of the reasons I allowed him to kiss me at all." She glanced at Finn. "Although if you let that compliment go to your head, so help me, you'll have twin duty for a month, and I'll encourage them to use you as target practice."

"Well, seeing as I'm so charming, I may be able to sweet talk you out of it..." Arabella narrowed her eyes and he chuckled. "I may wait to test out that theory for a later time, though. The doctor should clear you in the next few weeks, and I fully plan to foist off our offspring on my aunt and have you for an entire night to myself."

Freya burped, and Arabella held her out to Finn to exchange babies. As soon as she had Declan nursing, she met his gaze again. "You want sex, you know what you need to do. I'm not having any more children."

His dragon huffed. *Why do we have to be snipped? That's what birth control is for.*

Aye, but it's not a guarantee.

Finn replied, "Let me work on handling my family first."

"You do know it takes three months for it to be fully effective?"

"Aye, but I've been a bit busy."

Her face softened. "I know. If you have it done, I'll give you some leeway provided we do everything possible to prevent another pregnancy. I appreciate all the help, but three is a handful. I can only imagine what they'll be like when they're older."

"Especially if they take after your brother."

"It's more taking after you and your cousins that I'm worried about. The Stewart siblings will cause havoc unlike anything the world has ever seen."

He smiled. "I thought you didn't like hyperboles?"

"Usually. But in this case, it may not be."

As Freya drifted off, Finn gently laid her down in the bouncy seat and fastened the strap around her. "I'll schedule an appointment with Layla as soon as possible." He stood and ran a hand through his hair. "Now, what to do about my family."

"Talk with them, Finn. Honesty can go a long way. And if that doesn't work, give them orders. That's what clan leaders do."

He tapped his hand against his thigh. "It might help if we invite them here and you back me up. Hearing it from two people may be more convincing."

"Provided you convince Meg Boyd to babysit, then I'll help."

Meg Boyd was Aunt Lorna's frenemy and arguably the biggest gossip on Lochguard. "If she can ever tear herself away from her two beaus..."

Arabella grinned. "Oh, you know the entire clan is enjoying that one. If anyone was to lead along two males and put off a long-term relationship, it would be Meg."

"The only good thing from it all is that Archie and Cal have formed a temporary truce."

Archie and Cal were neighbors who usually tried to

sabotage one another through stealing sheep or dropping boulders on one another's barns. They took up enormous amounts of Finn's time since he had to listen to both sides and make decisions once or twice a week.

Or, had done. He secretly hoped Meg Boyd would keep them occupied for the foreseeable future and save Finn many a headache.

Arabella snorted. "Well, seeing as they're sleeping with the same female, they have to have a truce or risk hurting Meg. The bigger question is whether they're all sleeping together or if Meg is enjoying one and then the other."

"That, my dear Ara, is something I'd rather not know."

"I didn't pin you for a prude."

"When it comes to Meg Boyd, I like to think she's an asexual being who lives only to hand out unwarranted advice. Now let's get the last lad fed and start arranging the family dinner."

As they finished taking care of their children, Finn began to plan the next evening with his cousins and their mates. Arabella was right, as she usually was. He needed to be honest and lay out the facts.

His dragon spoke up. *Good luck with that. Make sure to hide all the valuables.*

I'm sure they're not going to start throwing breakables.

Do you know them at all?

With Holly and Faye both being pregnant, everyone will be a bit more careful.

If they don't shout and startle Holly into labor first.

Not wanting to think of all the ways the dinner could go wrong, as soon as the bairns were down again, Finn pulled Arabella up against his side and cupped her cheek. "I love you, Ara."

She searched his eyes. "What do you want?"

"Nothing." He nuzzled her cheek with his. "I just don't

say it enough."

Before she could question him further, he kissed her. As he tasted and stroked the inside of his mate's mouth, Finn temporarily forgot about the rest of his problems. No matter what happened, he would always have Arabella and his children. And at the end of the day, that was the greatest prize of all.

Chapter Two

The next evening, Arabella MacLeod walked into her dining room and quietly took her seat. As the MacKenzies often did when in the home of a family member, they ignored everyone around them to argue and bicker with one another.

Faye, the youngest one with wild, curly brown hair, pointed a finger at her brother Fraser. "Just leave Holly alone, brother. Why you think breathing will break every bone in her body, I'll never understand."

Fraser stopped fussing with his mate Holly to look at his younger sister and narrow his blue eyes. "Don't be ridiculous. She needs to breathe to stay alive. These chairs are bloody uncomfortable, and Holly's having a hard enough time as it is."

Holly opened her mouth, but Faye cut her off. "The chairs are fine, and you know it. Keep it up, and she'll leave you the first chance she gets."

Holly mumbled, "If I haven't left yet, I'm not going anywhere." However, neither MacKenzie heard her.

Fraser growled at his sister. "When you're nearly nine months pregnant, then you can tell me how bloody comfortable these chairs are, sister. Until then, you have no say."

"And you do? Did you grow a uterus I was unaware of and magically become nine months pregnant? Because if so, then you must be having gnomes for children with a flat belly like that."

Holly glanced at Arabella and rolled her eyes. Arabella smiled back in understanding. Fraser and Finn were the most alike between the cousins, and much like how Arabella helped to steady Finn at times, Holly did the same with Fraser.

Her dragon spoke up. *The difference is that Fraser acts like a teenager most of the time.*

Now, now, that's unfair. He's done a bit of maturing since meeting Holly.

He'll never compare to our Finn.

I'll agree with that much, dragon.

The last remaining MacKenzie sibling, Fergus, stood and paced the length of the room and back again. His mate, Gina, sighed. "Sit down, Fergus. Pacing only makes your dragon more anxious."

She reached up to touch him, but Fergus moved away. "I'm sorry, lass. I want to sit down and put my arm around you, but my beast is walking a fine line."

Faye jumped in. "Have the blasted frenzy, Fergus. Gina's said that she's ready more times than I can count."

Fergus shook his head. "Wee Jamie isn't even a year old. That's not enough time."

Gina stood. "Fergus, shouldn't I have the final say when I'm ready? Your caring for others and my needs is one of the reasons I love you, but you need to listen to me on this. If you don't do something soon, you could end up losing your job, not to mention me, too."

He frowned. "What are you talking about?"

"Seeing you suffer like this, day in and day out, is killing me, Fergus. I need my steadfast mate at my side. Either let the frenzy take place, or I'm going to move in with my sister."

Fergus's brows furrowed, and Arabella sensed he was about to be overly dutiful and ruin everything. She'd wanted to wait until Finn brought in the food before she said anything, but it could be too late by then.

Arabella put every bit of dominance into her voice she could muster. "Listen to your mate, Fergus. Because if you don't, you're a fool."

Six pairs of eyes turned toward her. At one point in her life, Arabella would've run away from such scrutiny. But the MacKenzies were her family now. And she wasn't about to shirk from healing and helping them any way she could. She continued, "Go on, stare at me. Glower, even. But Gina is all but throwing herself at you, Fergus. If you don't take her, then you don't deserve her."

Fergus growled. "Watch it, Ara."

She raised an eyebrow. "Why? Because it's the truth and it hurts? I'm not afraid of you, Fergus. And if you think I'm going to sit and say nothing, then you don't know me at all." She switched her gaze to Gina. "Am I right? You want the frenzy?" Gina nodded, and Arabella looked back at Fergus. "Then go. Tonight."

Gina shook her head. "As much as I want to, we can't. There's no one to watch Jamie."

Arabella flicked a hand toward Faye and her mate, Grant. "They can watch him."

Faye blinked. "What?"

Shrugging a shoulder, Arabella said, "You're about to become parents yourself before too long, and it'll be good practice. Besides, Grant's mum can help, too. She loves children. All in all, it's perfect."

Grant, the silent one with everyone but his mate, finally spoke up. "We can do it, Faye. It'll be good preparation and it'll help your brother."

"You mean it'll be good practice for me as I'm sure I'll be the one watching him," Faye muttered.

Grant took Faye's chin between his fingers. "No, we will do it together. We share our Protector duties and we'll share bairn duties. Mum can watch him when need be."

Faye shifted in her seat and mumbled, "I suppose so."

Arabella focused back on Gina and Fergus. "Right, then go home and pack everything up for Mac-squared. Faye and Grant will follow you shortly so they can take everything to their cottage."

Mac-squared was the nickname for wee Jamie MacDonald-MacKenzie, Gina's son that had been adopted by Fergus at birth. Even Arabella couldn't help but use it since it irritated Fergus.

Gina glanced at Fergus. "Well? What do you say?"

He took a step toward her. "Are you truly ready for this, love?"

Gina bobbed her head. "Yes. I miss holding and kissing my mate. I knew a frenzy was in my future when I mated you, Fergus. Please believe me when I say I'm more than ready."

Letting out a long breath, Fergus took Gina's hand and pulled her up. "Right, then let's get a move on. My dragon has agreed to relax for an hour to get everything sorted. So let's make the most of it."

Gina mouthed, "Thank you" to Arabella as they exited the room.

Not wanting to give Faye and Grant the opportunity to leave just yet, she pierced them with her gaze again. "And now you, Faye MacKenzie."

Faye's brows furrowed. "What did I do?"

"I understand hormones messing with your moods during pregnancy, especially when it comes to irritation.

But throwing dishes at Grant in a restaurant is going a bit too far."

She sighed. "You heard about that."

"Everyone has heard about it," Arabella pointed out. "The question is, what can you do to contain your outbursts? It's not fair to the clan for them to have to lock up their breakables when you visit one of their businesses or homes. Something needs to be done."

Faye glanced at her mate. "If Grant gave me more work to do, it'd keep me out of trouble."

Grant grunted. "I'm not about to send you on patrols."

Arabella shook her head. "Faye's what, two or so months along? If Finn let me fly until I was nearly six months pregnant with triplets, Grant should be able to handle two months with whatever amount of children she's carrying."

Faye muttered, "It's two."

Holly grinned. "I knew it! It's the MacKenzie curse-slash-blessing."

Fraser added, "Ours will be older, though, so your children will have to listen to ours."

Faye rolled her eyes. "I announce I'm carrying twins and you respond by laying out the hierarchy of our unborn children?"

Thrusting out his chest, Fraser nodded. "Too right, I do. It'll give you more time to get used to the idea."

Faye stood. "Fraser MacKenzie, if you think I'm going to allow your children to lead mine into trouble, you must've been hit in the head one too many times."

Holly stood. "Enough. You two have plenty of time to argue about whose children will be leading the others into trouble. Right now, we should congratulate Faye and Grant."

Finn finally came into the room. "Congratulate what?"

Faye growled. "You can hear well enough in the kitchen,

unless you're losing your hearing, old man."

Finn wrapped Faye in a hug and released her. "All I can say is good luck."

Arabella sighed. "And to think you complained about everyone teasing you before the triplets were born."

He shrugged. "Teasing is what we do and complaining about it is just a formality."

Finn came up to Arabella and kissed her gently before whispering, "Nice work with Fergus and Gina."

"You were taking too bloody long, so I handled it. Although I suspect you were hovering in the kitchen on purpose."

He squeezed her side. "I think you're going to be our children's version of Aunt Lorna, the female who can handle anything."

"If I can handle you and your family, then I *can* handle anything," she said with a smile. After kissing Finn, she looked back at Faye. "We'll have a proper celebration later. But right now, Fergus and Gina need you."

Nodding, Faye took Grant's hand. "I may have to call about a few things, what with my mum being out of town."

"Anytime, Faye," Arabella replied. "And call my mobile; otherwise, I'm sure Finn will purposely give you the worst possible advice to make your life miserable."

Finn interjected, "Now, now, it wouldn't be anything life-threatening. But if a bairn starts crying, play loud music. That always helps, especially if it's metal."

Arabella lightly hit his side. "Don't listen to him. Call me or risk an endless night of crying. Because, apparently, Finn is willing to upset his nephew for his own prank."

"I wouldn't tell them that in reality, Ara."

She glanced at him and shook her head.

Grant spoke up. "We'll be off, then."

As Faye and Grant exited the dining room, Arabella sat

down. "Well? Where's our food, Finn? I hope you have something to show for your eavesdropping from the kitchen."

He winked. "Aye, I'll fetch it."

With Faye gone, Fraser went back to fussing over Holly. "Would you rather sit in my lap, love? Or I can find a pillow."

Holly smiled at her mate and touched his cheek. "I'm fine, Fraser. Females have endured pregnancy since the beginning of time. Sitting in a hard chair is hardly a trial."

"But it's unnecessary. This isn't the Dark Ages."

Before Holly could respond, Finn returned carrying a large bowl of what smelled like curry. He set it down. "I know it's not fish and chips, but I thought curry might help Holly along. I made it extra spicy."

Fraser frowned, but Holly placed a hand on his bicep. "I'm due in the next few weeks, Fraser. At this point, I prefer labor to any more arguments about my comfort level."

He took her hand and kissed the back of it. "Has it really been that bad, honey? I just want to ensure everything goes smoothly, unlike the last time."

She cupped his cheek. "Oh, Fraser. The bairns and I are fine. I wish you'd stop worrying."

"I don't think I ever will."

Holly caressed his jaw with her fingers. "Then congratulations, you're feeling like a parent."

Arabella added, "Besides, Holly's been receiving dragon's blood injections. If her theory is correct, childbirth should be easier as a result."

In the past, humans had had a fifty-fifty chance of dying when birthing a half-dragon-shifter child. Holly was determined to change that, and Arabella only hoped she succeeded.

Holly nodded. "Aye, and since I'll be the first human test

subject to give birth, it'll be important for many reasons."

Fraser murmured, "But you giving me two children is more important than anything."

After kissing Fraser, Holly leaned back just as Finn brought in the rice and naan. Once everyone had food, they dug in.

Finn was the first to speak again. "Fraser, I have loads of people asking when you'll be tackling your next project. When will that be?"

Holly answered, "Never, if he had his way. Maybe you should order him to do so."

Fraser swallowed his food. "That is quite spicy, cousin." He took a drink and continued, "My family is my priority."

"As it should be," Finn answered. "But you're the clan's architect. Human ones won't work with us, and reaching out to other clans will take time. The DDA and local human oversight agencies are familiar with your work, Fraser. The clan needs you, too."

Arabella chimed in. "Besides, don't you want to leave behind legacies to show off to your children when they're older? I believe the school is one of the places waiting for your services. That's something that will directly impact your family."

"Laying it on thick, aren't you, Arabella?" Fraser drawled.

She shrugged. "Asking hasn't worked and tying you up won't accomplish anything. So, guilt-tripping seems the best option. I'm sure Aunt Lorna would approve."

Finn snorted. "We've definitely rubbed off on you."

"I have three children with your blood and genes. If I don't adapt, I'll be held hostage within a matter of years by our three rebels."

Finn opened his mouth to reply, but Holly sucked in her breath. All eyes moved to her, but Fraser asked, "Is everything okay?"

"For once, your worry is warranted. My water just broke. It seems Finn's curry did the trick."

Fraser jumped up. "Then we need to get you to the surgery. Finn, will you call Stonefire and have Gregor and Sid come, too? I want the best care for my mate."

Arabella's dragon snorted. *That's going a bit overboard.*

Ignoring her beast, she stood. "I'll call Stonefire. Finn, you help Fraser get Holly to the surgery."

Finn didn't argue, but merely grunted his assent and went to his cousin's aid.

Arabella had hoped to solve all the MacKenzie issues at dinner, but she hadn't counted on Holly going into labor as well.

Her dragon spoke up. *It just shows that we're good at keeping them in line.*

Yes, because I have magical powers over inducing labor, she drawled.

Maybe. We'll have to try again with Faye.

Are you done? I need to call Bram.

And what about Aunt Lorna and Ross? her beast asked.

One thing at a time, dragon. I have to sort out our own children as well. Meg can't watch them forever.

Rushing out of the room, Arabella found her mobile phone and dialed Stonefire's leader, Bram Moore-Llewelyn. He answered, "Arabella? What's happening?"

"Well..." She explained the situation and hoped her former clan leader wouldn't think her daft for making the call. Three doctors was a bit much, but Fraser and Holly were family. And no matter how much they may irritate her on occasion, she loved them and would do whatever she could to protect them.

CHAPTER THREE

When Finn and Fraser finally got Holly to the surgery, there was a problem. Finn frowned. "What do you mean Layla is busy with another delivery?"

The nurse at reception, Tyler MacPherson, merely raised an eyebrow. "Your hearing works fine, Finn. Hamish Boyd's mate went into labor about five hours ago. However, she still hasn't delivered, and seeing as it's her first, it may be a while yet. Dr. MacFie is with her now."

Fraser ran a hand through his hair. "Poor timing on the Boyds' part."

Holly tsked at her mate. "I'm far from delivering at this point, Fraser. Besides, it's not as if Alba Boyd can time when she goes into labor. I've been checking in on her over the last eight and a half months, and she's lovely, if not a bit quiet." She looked back at Tyler. "Just put me in a room and have Logan check on me. We'll be fine for the foreseeable future. I've helped deliver a fair few bairns and know the drill."

Logan Lamont was one of Lochguard's nurses, who had been working with Holly on her dragon's blood research project.

As soon as Holly settled ungracefully into a wheelchair, Fraser wheeled her to the room she wanted. Once his cousins were out of sight, Finn turned back to Tyler. "So if Hamish and Alba Boyd are having a baby, then where's Meg Boyd? She wouldn't miss her latest grandchild's debut."

An older female's voice sounded behind him. "I'm right here, Finlay."

Turning slowly, Finn found Meg holding his daughter. To either side of her was one of her beaus, holding one of his sons each.

He closed the distance to the group. "Why didn't you call me?"

She shrugged. "You were busy, and besides, it'll be some time before Alba delivers my grandchild. Archie and Cal don't have any grandkids yet, so they were all too willing to come with me."

As each male looked at Meg with adoration, Finn started to think the rumors about all three of them being in a relationship were true.

He quickly took Freya from Meg and held his daughter close. "Where are the rest of your brood?"

Meg waved a hand in dismissal. "Alistair's doing some sort of research and said he'll come once the bairn is here. Graham is with his mate and children, and should be here soon. Unlike Lorna, I didn't go on my honeymoon at the same time as when one of my daughters-in-law were due. I'll have my whole family here for the event. I'm hoping we finally have a female Boyd. I love my sons and grandsons, but I could do with a wee girl to pass on my secrets."

Finn resisted pinching the bridge of his nose. "I ordered my aunt to take a holiday, Meg." And he decided to push the one angle that would drive the older female crazy. "After all, she managed to get all her children mated, and that can tire out a person."

Meg huffed. "Alistair is stubborn, like his father. Him being single isn't my problem any longer."

He raised an eyebrow. "I thought you always said it was the greatest duty of a mother to see her children mated."

Raising her head, Meg opened her mouth, but Arabella rushed into the surgery at that moment. In the blink of an eye, she had Declan on one hip and Grayson on the other. After kissing each of them, she smiled at Meg. "Thanks for watching them, Meg. You're the auntie they like best."

Finn bit his lip to keep from laughing. Arabella MacLeod had indeed come a long way if she were flattering the old biddy.

His dragon spoke up. *She had to. You've become cranky with so little sleep.*

Me? We're one and the same, dragon.

I at least have the sense not to irritate Meg Boyd. That could backfire spectacularly later on.

Hush.

Arabella moved to Finn's side. "Dr. Lewis agreed to watch over Stonefire, so Sid and Gregor should be here in about an hour."

Dr. Trahern Lewis was a junior doctor on Stonefire who usually preferred to stay sequestered in a research lab. Finn wondered how Arabella had managed that one.

Meg jumped in. "Why does Holly get two or three doctors and my Hamish's Alba only one?"

Finn kept his tone patient. "Because Holly is not only human, she's also having twins. Extra doctors seems reasonable, aye?"

"I suppose." Meg looked at Cal and Archie in turn. "Let's go check on how Alba's doing."

Arabella murmured an additional thank-you. Once the trio were gone, she smiled up at him. "You shouldn't let Meg get to you."

"She insulted Aunt Lorna."

"When does she not?"

"Fair point." Freya wiggled in his arms, and he turned his attention to his daughter. "Did Auntie Meg not play with you?" He lifted Freya up, down, and up again. "After all, dragon-shifters like to be in the sky now and again. Although we'll have to wait a few years before you go much higher, aye?"

Bringing her down, he gave Freya a sloppy kiss and settled her against his chest again. "I want to be here for Fraser and Holly, but keeping the bairns in the reception area won't be easy."

Tyler spoke up from behind them. "While it's not quite finished, Dr. MacFie's been having a playroom and nursery put together. There are a few cribs as well as toys. You can wait there, if you like."

He glanced at Arabella. "Is that all right, love?"

She nodded. "Of course. Holly and Fraser might need us, and the triplets don't mind where they sleep and eat as long as they do."

Arabella referred to the fact that since Holly was human, she had an increased risk of dying during delivery.

His dragon grunted. *But she's had quite a bit of Fraser's blood injected into her. She'll do fine.*

Even dragon-shifters die in childbirth, dragon. You know that. Remember Gregor's first mate?

His beast huffed. *But it won't happen to Holly. She's strong and will fight with everything she has to be there for her children.*

Holly's mother had been murdered a number of years ago. The lass still mourned her.

Fraser looked back to Tyler. "Aye, that'll do, Tyler. Show us the way."

He picked up the nappy bags Meg had brought with her. As Tyler guided them down the hallway, Arabella said, "I also called Faye and Grant before coming here. We all decided not to tell Fergus and Gina about Holly going into labor, or they may never start the frenzy."

"Aye, that's the decision I would've made, too. Especially if there's a complication, then Fergus's dragon could lose it and go rogue. I'm sure Fraser will forgive him for missing his children's birth if it means keeping his brother sane and whole."

Tyler stopped in front of a room. "Here you are. I'll keep you updated on Holly and Fraser. There's a phone in the room, and it'll ring when we have updates. That way I won't tie up your mobile in case there's a clan emergency."

Finn patted the nurse's arm. "Thanks, Tyler."

Tyler nodded. Arabella and Finn entered the play-room-slash-nursery.

The bright colors on the walls were painted in geometric designs, and the white cribs were lined to one side. Bins of toys were stacked in one corner, and a number of comfy armchairs were scattered about the room. There was even a gliding chair nestled in the darkest corner of the room, probably to help with getting a bairn to sleep or even with nursing.

Finn whistled. "As much as I love Gregor, the surgery has definitely improved under a female's touch."

Arabella placed the boys in a crib and gave each a stuffed toy. "Layla MacFie is more likely to think about babies, parents, and their needs. Gregor always tried to block them out, because of how his mate and unborn baby died in childbirth."

Finn placed Freya next to her two brothers. "Aye, but he has a bairn on the way now with Sid, so I expect that will change."

Fishing out Freya's favorite stuffed fox, he laid it next to her. After kissing each of his children on the forehead, he whispered, "You lot look sleepy. Maybe if you cooperate with Mummy and Daddy and take a nap, then we'll have time to think of some fun games later on."

Declan moved his head and lightly banged it against his brother.

With a sigh, Finn created a stuffed toy wall between each of them. When outside their home, the triplets preferred sleeping in one bed. Separating them could end in hours of frustration for all involved.

He could only imagine what would happen if their tendency to stick together endured into their teen years. Finn would probably go completely gray.

His dragon sighed. *Stop complaining. You look forward to it.*

You might, but I remember what we were like. And there was only one of us and we have three of the little buggers.

Arabella will help and it will be enough.

Scanning the room, Finn located a lullaby toy. Pressing the button, it played a soothing melody.

Freya yawned first, followed quickly by her brothers. He held his breath, hoping that Meg and her males had tired them out.

As each slowly closed their eyes, he exhaled. He kept his voice low as he said to Arabella, "Thank you for earlier, love. Sometimes I wonder if you should've been made clan leader instead of me."

She whispered back, "Putting aside I was in England at the time of the trials, barely speaking to anyone, I still say no, thank you. Besides, you don't need to thank me for merely acting as your mate."

He shook his head. "Don't downplay your importance, Ara. I won't have it."

Leaning against him, she murmured, "Fine. I *am* fairly brilliant. But you've been having a hard time, and since you were there for me when I needed it most, I'm trying to do the same."

He kissed her forehead. "I love you, Arabella MacLeod."

"I love you, too, Finlay Stewart."

They stood in silence for several minutes, watching their children sleep.

His dragon spoke up. *I love Aunt Lorna, but I wish our parents could be here, too.*

Aye, I know, dragon. But raising these three hellions will help keep their legacy alive.

Finn's father had been clan leader many years ago, but he and Finn's mother had died at the hands of enemies when Finn had been a teenager.

His beast replied, *I think it's time to revisit Ara's idea.*

I think you're right.

He whispered, "Once all of this is sorted, I want to help you make the picture family tree in the living room."

She glanced up. "Are you sure? I know having your parents' pictures on the wall won't be easy."

He squeezed her waist. "It'll be just as difficult for you, doing it with your parents, Ara, and yet you're willing to hang them up."

She ran her hand up and down his side. "My mother saved my life. The least I can do is keep her memory alive for our children. Besides, having pictures of both your mother and mine will help Freya understand why I gave her the middle names of Anne and Jocelyn."

Anne had been his mum's name and Jocelyn had been Arabella's mother's name.

He gently squeezed her shoulders. "And your father? After all, our sons each carry the names of one of their grandfathers. Can you handle having his picture on the wall, too?"

"I—" She paused and finally continued, "I hate the unknowing, but I think it's finally time to accept that my father is dead. He disappeared not long after my mum died and never returned. If Kai and Bram haven't been able to find him, then he's gone for good. Having his picture around will help me accept that fact."

"Then I suppose it's time for both of us to push past the pain so our children can better know their grandparents."

"I hope we can be around longer than either of our parents were, so that our children don't have to go through the same pain so young in life," Arabella whispered.

He pulled Arabella tighter against his side. "As I've said, I'm going to do everything within my power to ensure our three hellions have us for a very long time."

As he memorized his sleeping children's faces, a sense of peace washed over Finn. True, something could go wrong soon enough, but these were the moments he'd use to draw strength and fight for every one of his clan members' future.

Chapter Four

A baby's cry woke up Arabella. Blinking her eyes open, she tugged at Finn's arm around her waist, and he released her.

She quickly reached the crib, but stopped breathing at what she saw. Freya was awake, but her pupils were slitted.

Which meant her inner dragon was either in charge or talking with Freya.

Her dragon spoke up. *That shouldn't happen yet.*

Keeping her voice low and as free of panic as she should, she said, "Finn, wake up."

He grumbled, and Arabella debated whether to pick up her daughter or not. If Freya's dragon had somehow managed to take control, she didn't want to push the beast too far and possibly cause it to go rogue.

Which meant she might lose her daughter forever.

"What is it?" Finn asked on a yawn.

Arabella pointed at Freya and Finn leaned forward, clearly alert. "What the...?"

She kept her tone low and light, so as to not upset Freya. "What do we do, Finn? That's not normal. She's only a few months old. Her dragon shouldn't speak to her until five years at the earliest."

"I don't know. But maybe Layla or Logan might. Let me

see."

After quickly squeezing her shoulder, Finn raced out of the room.

The second her father was out of sight, Freya began crying. The sight of her pink-faced baby with tears rolling down her cheeks tugged at Arabella's heart. No doubt, she was scared and confused. "Sssh, Freya, love. Daddy's getting us some help. We'll have this sorted soon enough."

Freya didn't exactly settle, but at least she merely sniffled instead of bawled.

Arabella glanced at the twins. Declan slept through anything, but Grayson stirred a little and would soon join his sister's cries.

It was Arabella's job to protect her babies, and yet, all she could do was stand and watch or risk making things worse.

She said to her dragon, *I hate not knowing what to do.*

There has to be a reason for why this happened to Freya now. Young dragons must be provoked into coming out of their hiding spots inside their minds this early.

Layla raced into the room, with Finn close on her heels. The doctor stopped at the crib and studied Freya's eyes. After a few beats, Layla spoke in her stern, yet gentle doctor voice filled with dominance. "Now, now, I know your dragon must be impatient to come out to play, but she really should be sleeping somewhere safe in your mind."

Freya's soft cries turned into what Arabella could only describe as roars.

Grayson started wailing, but thankfully, his pupils were round. Finn swiftly picked up their son and carried him to the other side of the room to calm him.

Arabella glanced at the doctor. "What do we do, Layla? Have you seen it before?"

Layla kept her voice gentle. "Only in textbooks. But Sid

and Gregor just arrived, and if anyone can help with unusual inner dragon-related problems, it's them."

Dr. Sid had lost her dragon for twenty years, until Gregor had brought out her beast during the mate-claim frenzy. Ever since then, Gregor had dedicated his free time to learning as much as possible about inner dragons and how they worked. While not a guaranteed solution, Arabella had faith that Sid and Gregor could help or find a way to do so.

Arabella reached for Freya, but quickly clenched her fingers into a fist. She still didn't know if picking her daughter up would make things worse. "It's all right, Freya. Mummy's old friend, Dr. Sid, will be coming soon. She and her mate might be able to help you."

Layla went to the door and shouted something to a nurse about bringing the Stonefire doctors to the nursery. She then dashed back inside. "Is there anything that could've caused this? Finn didn't think so, but I wanted to double-check with you, too."

Arabella ran through the day and shook her head. "No, the only difference in the routine today was that Meg watched the triplets for a bit."

Finn grunted. "I'm going to ask Meg what she did with them."

Noticing the blame in Finn's voice, she said, "Finn, don't shout at her. For all we know, she didn't do anything wrong, and Freya's dragon did this on her own."

Layla nodded. "Ara's right. Meg will be in Room 3 with her new grandson. Try not to ruin the happy moment for them all."

Finn grunted, his voice a little less accusatory. "Aye, I'll try not to. Although if she begins one of her guilt trips about Aunt Lorna, I can't make any promises. This is too important."

Finn disappeared with Grayson still in his arms and Arabella turned back to Freya. She searched for her daughter's favorite fox toy but didn't spot it in the crib. Spotting it on the floor, she risked giving the toy to Freya. The second the fox was next to her, Freya stopped crying and her pupils returned to round again.

"I don't understand," Arabella stated. "Her dragon wanted the toy? Why go to all that trouble?"

Layla shook her head. "I have no idea. But if Freya's dragon is active at this young of an age, we're all going to have to tread carefully. We can't exactly teach a bairn how to control an inner beast."

Sid and Gregor rushed through the door. Gregor asked, "What's wrong, Layla? They simply said to hurry here."

Layla turned toward her former mentor with a frown. "I'm not sure. Freya's pupils were slitted and I swear she roared."

Gregor moved to the crib. "She looks content and back to normal now."

Arabella filled him in on the details and added, "Once she had her favorite toy again, her pupils returned to normal. Is there anything you can tell us, Gregor? Please?"

Sid appeared on Arabella's other side and she placed a hand on her shoulder. "Let us take a look first, Ara. And then we'll go from there."

Arabella nodded and stepped back. She never tore her gaze from her daughter as Layla said, "I need to check on Holly. Will you be fine with Sid and Gregor here?"

Arabella murmured her assurance.

"Aye, then I'll be back as soon as I can."

Clasping her hands, Arabella tried her best to stay calm.

Her beast spoke up. *I think Freya will be fine. Her dragon must be anxious to come out and play.*

But at that age, the dragon could easily overpower her, and we'll lose our baby girl. Few children under the age of five whose dragons take control resist going rogue. And even fewer ever return to their former selves.

Any children born to us and Finn are guaranteed to be stubborn. I believe in Freya. She'll find a way.

Finn returned and instantly moved to her side. Once he wrapped his arm around her shoulders, she leaned into him and placed a hand on Grayson's back. The combined warmth of the two males helped her to relax a fraction. "Did you learn anything from Meg?"

"The only thing out of the ordinary is that the twins drank all of your breast milk and she had to give Freya some of the formula Graham's mate uses for his son. But Graham's son has never had flashing dragon eyes, so I'm not sure it's related."

Gregor joined them. "It could be. If Freya's allergic to something in the formula, it's possible it brought out her dragon. Whilst allergies are rare for dragon-shifters, an allergic reaction could've affected her inner dragon to such an extent it left the hibernation area of the mind."

Arabella forced her voice to remain calm for her son's sake. "What can we do?"

"I'll run a series of tests to see if I can determine the cause," Gregor answered. "The allergy must be minor, as I didn't see any physical manifestations related to it, such as swelling or rashes. However, I'm not sure if the effect will be long-term or not. It depends on genetics and the individual dragon-shifter. Has anyone in either of your families had allergic reactions before?"

Arabella nodded. "My father did, although I'm not sure what it was. Finn? What about yours?"

He shook his head. "No, my parents didn't have allergies, nor do any of my extended family."

She leaned more against Finn. "I think we need to call Tristan. He's older and always spent more time with Dad than Mum before he disappeared. He might know the specifics of our father's allergies."

Sid jumped in. "I'll call Trahern first to check our records and then talk with Tristan. Right now, the best thing you can do is cuddle your daughter. Gregor will stay here, in case anything happens."

Without missing a beat, Arabella rushed to scoop up her daughter, careful to keep the little stuffed fox with her.

Hugging her close, she breathed in her baby's scent and murmured, "We'll sort this out, Freya." She kissed the top of her head. "Mummy and Daddy will do whatever we can to help."

Although even that might not be enough.

Her beast growled. *Stop it. Freya needs our support.*

I've never been a full-blown optimist, dragon. You know that.

Then try it. Otherwise, you're all but giving up.

Arabella was about to refute her dragon's claims, but Gregor's voice filled the room. "That lad can sleep. I hope my bairn is like that."

Finn never stopped rubbing Grayson's back in soothing motions as he turned his gaze toward Declan. "Aye, unless his brother picks on him in his sleep, then he wakes up."

Arabella forced a smile, but as Finn and Gregor joked about Declan sleeping through an atomic bomb, Arabella merely sat in the glider and rocked her daughter until she fell asleep.

She hoped that Dr. Sid could find the answers they needed concerning Arabella's father because the thought of losing her only daughter forever to a rogue inner dragon was unthinkable.

No. Arabella had lost so much already—her mother, father, and even a decade of her life after the dragon hunters had tortured her, when she'd avoided everyone and shut in on herself.

There was no way she was going to lose any of her children. If Dr. Sid and Tristan couldn't help with determining her dad's allergies, then Arabella would do something she swore she'd never do again—go looking in the darkest corners of the internet for information related to her father.

~~~

Finn tried his best to lighten the mood by joking with Gregor. But watching Arabella as she held and rocked their daughter as if it could be the last time she'd ever do so sat heavy in his heart. After everything his mate had been through with the fucking dragon hunters, she deserved a happy life, free of more grief.

His dragon spoke up. *She is happy most of the time.*

But not now. And there's not a bloody thing I can do about it.

Dr. Sid is a good doctor. She and Gregor will sort it out.

He wanted to be optimistic, but as clan leader, his brain didn't always work like that. He preferred searching for concrete evidence and solutions.

Gregor's voice garnered his attention. "If Cassidy can't find what she needs, then I'll start asking all the doctors involved in my information project."

Gregor was the only one who called Dr. Sid by her full name, Cassidy.

The doctor couple had decided that they didn't like how dragon-shifters lacked any central medical association or authority to store and share information. So in recent months, Gregor had started working to form his own, with Sid helping when possible. Finn had also given Layla permission to contribute when she could.

Finn nodded. "Aye, I know you will do everything within
~~~

your power to help us, Gregor." He glanced again at Arabella in the glider chair, holding Freya close as she sang her a lullaby. "I've been putting off finding another doctor to help out Layla, but once my daughter is safe again, then I'll move it to the top of my list. That way, Lochguard can contribute more to your project and hopefully we can help other children in need. I'm sure Freya isn't the only case."

"Even from what little I've been able to accomplish, I've heard of other bairns waking up with slitted pupils. In those cases, it was a result of trauma or having one or both of their parents die. That's not the case here, but as soon as I learn anything relevant, I'll tell you straight away, Finn."

"Thanks, Gregor."

The doctor wandered to the other side of the room and pulled out his mobile phone, no doubt to get to work and give Finn and Arabella some privacy.

Glancing down at his sleeping son, Finn decided to lay him in the crib next to his still sleeping brother. Just as he was about to go to Arabella's side, Sid came back into the room. He asked, "Well?"

She shook her head. "The doctor before me did a poor job at preserving records and half of them were unreadable due to a broken water pipe a decade ago. Tristan didn't know of anything either, but says he might be able to find out."

He frowned. "How? George MacLeod disappeared without a trace years ago."

Sid shrugged. "He said he'll call me as soon as he can. For now, I'd suggest keeping Freya here in case her dragon reappears. That way, Gregor or I can observe and formulate ideas to help."

He wanted to scream that an idea wasn't good enough, but Finn restrained himself.

Arabella spoke up from the corner. "What about Holly? How is she?"

Despite everything, his mate still cared about his family. He couldn't imagine a better female to call his own.

Sid inserted her hands into the pockets of her lab coat. "She's still in labor, but nothing out of the ordinary. While it's still too early to tell definitively, the dragon's blood seems to be helping her."

Gregor looked up from his phone. "And just remember that I'm no longer your clan member to scold, aye? But I asked Tyler to call Aunt Lorna."

Arabella spoke up from the corner. "Good. She should be here." She met Finn's gaze. "Not because I don't think you're capable, because you're a brilliant clan leader. But she is family and deserves to be here with us, to celebrate Holly."

And enjoy Freya while she still can was left unsaid.

Although if Finn had anything to do with it, his daughter would live a long life, complete with a mentally stable inner dragon.

His beast spoke up. *Saying it doesn't make it true.*

Aye, but I've barely begun. If I have to call in every favor I have with the dragon-shifters in the UK and Ireland, I will.

Moving to Arabella's side, he stared at Freya's sleeping face. "I hate to admit you're right, but you are, Ara. Aunt Lorna keeps us all grounded."

He placed his hand on Arabella's shoulder and she covered it with her own. This latest development was a test. But he and Arabella were strong and would win this battle. Finn was sure of it.

Chapter Five

Arabella had just finished feeding her babies again and gotten them back to sleep when Faye and Grant entered the nursery, little Mac-squared squirming in Grant's arms.

Making a motion to be quiet, she walked up to them and whispered, "What are you doing here? I told Finn that you should stay home. There's no reason for everyone to sleep on cots and the floor."

Faye raised her brows. "If you think sleeping on the floor is going to keep me away from supporting my cousins and little Freya, then you must be exhausted and without all your sense." She engulfed Arabella in a hug. "If you need a break, Grant can watch them all for a few minutes whilst we nab some coffee."

Releasing Faye, Arabella smiled. "No, I'm fine. They're sleeping, after all. It's once they wake up that it becomes a madhouse."

Bouncing Mac-squared, Grant grunted quietly. "We'll help when they do, even if Finn returns by then from his important clan matter. Besides, wee Jamie here loves his cousins, and will help keep Freya occupied."

Arabella reached out and took Mac-squared's hand. "He's just started to crawl. If he does that in front of Freya, her dragon might get jealous and come out."

Faye patted the bag slung on her hip. "I brought all of Freya's favorite toys and books. I'm sure we can mollify the wee beastie."

She smiled. "Thanks, Faye. I know you have doubts about becoming a mother, but based on today, I think you'll do just fine."

Waving a hand in dismissal, Faye replied, "We'll see. I may not be a mum yet, but a few of my own mother's ways have rubbed off on me."

"Too bad cooking wasn't one of them," Grant murmured as humor danced in his eyes.

Faye stuck out her tongue. "I'll leave that to you. Besides, I'll be the food source before much longer, once the bairns are born. And it'll be your duty to feed me properly."

Mac-squared babbled, and Grant readjusted his grip on the baby. "I'll take wee Jamie with me to check on Holly and Fraser. That way we don't wake the triplets." Grant gently kissed Faye. "I'll even bring you back a scone with clotted cream."

Faye sighed. "While not my mum's, any scone is better than none."

Shaking his head, Grant exited the room. Faye didn't miss a beat in wrapping an arm around Arabella's waist and guiding her toward a plush chair. "You need to rest. If either of the lads wake up, I'll tend to them. And I'll only wake you if Freya's pupils turn slitted again."

"I'm fine—"

"Don't say you're fine. I know you think you always need to be strong, Ara, but even a clan leader's mate sometimes needs to let an emotion or two peek through."

She allowed Faye to guide her to the chair and she sat down. "To be honest, the emotions wanting out at this point are uncertainty and fear."

Arabella paused, wondering if she should mention her past to Faye.

Her dragon growled. *We can trust Faye. She would never pity or belittle us.*

I know, but she has one image of us, and I'm afraid to break it.

That is partially what kept you from reaching out to me. Don't block others out. We have Finn and the MacKenzies. They are our family.

Taking a deep breath, the words spilled from her lips, "I've lost my mother and father. And, in a way, my brother, too. I love Finn and would never trade my place on Lochguard, but I miss Tristan sometimes. And if anything happens to one of my children, I'm not sure if I'll be able to cope. I tend to close in on myself when things get tough. Finn has been helping me to break the habit, but it could always come back."

Faye squatted so that she was eye level with Arabella. "We all have fears to face, but one thing is certain—the MacKenzies stand together, no matter what happens. Never hesitate in asking us for help. After all, you have to put up with Finn. And that is punishment enough."

She smiled. "He's not that bad."

Faye snorted. "I know. Fraser is worse." She winked. "But in all seriousness, I think of you as my sister, Ara. Promise me that you'll ask for help when you need it."

Sometimes Arabella forgot how much her life had changed in the past year. She'd gone from relying solely on herself to having more people care about her than she could count.

Her dragon stood tall. *And me.*

And yes, you too, love.

She nodded. "I'll try. I know you want me to say yes without hesitation, but I sometimes still have trouble with Finn.

Give me a few years and I'll be better at it, I'm sure."

"Aye, I think so, too." Faye stood and extracted Arabella's laptop from her bag. "I thought you might want this. I know you always like to fiddle with something on it when you have a spare minute at home."

Taking the slim laptop, Arabella placed it on her legs and laid a hand on the cover. Finn and the doctors had asked for a little time, but Arabella wasn't sure she could wait. Opening the computer, she booted it up. "Thanks, Faye. There are a few things I need to do, whilst I have the chance."

"While you do that, I'm going to close my eyes but keep my ears open." She yawned and settled into one of the other chairs. "Carrying Grant's bairns is going to make me a dull person by the end. I swear that I never have any energy."

"It'll get better, eventually. Although you'll have a new kind of exhaustion once they're born."

Faye closed her eyes. "Don't remind me."

As her cousin dozed, Arabella opened a new window on her laptop and hesitated. Could she handle finding out her father was truly dead?

Her beast spoke up. *Knowing is always better. Because if he's gone, we need to work on accepting it. Not just for our sakes, but for the children as well.*

Admitting her dragon was correct, Arabella typed in a web address and started searching. Even if her father was gone, she had another objective—to find out his allergies. Only then could she maybe help her daughter.

Finn stood inside the guard station posted just inside the clan's front gate and resisted pacing the space. To help contain his energy, he crossed his arms over his chest and looked at Shay and Zoe, two of his Protectors. "Shouldn't they be here by now?"

Zoe shook her head. "Tristan MacLeod is driving to Lochguard. And even speeding, it takes some time."

"I just wish he'd bloody well tell me why he had to come in person," Finn growled.

Shay grinned. "It's not every day you can tell your clan leader to have some patience."

Finn grunted. "Aye, and coming from you, the one with the notorious temper, is a hundred times worse."

Shay shrugged. "Maybe I've matured."

Zoe snorted. "Right, and I'm the Queen of England."

"Scotland would be better," Shay pointed out.

"Fine, how about Queen of Planet Earth?"

"Or, the galaxy?"

Finn sighed. "Are you sure you two are Protectors? I feel as if I'm back in secondary school."

"Well, you are older than us, so if you're in secondary school, we're in primary..." Shay began.

Uncrossing his arms, Finn put up a hand. "Just stop." He leaned toward the security monitor. "That has to be Tristan."

The two Protectors also looked at the security feed.

A dark sedan finally stopped in front of the gate and the feed switched to the driver's side window. Sure enough, Tristan's dark head and disgruntled brown eyes stared into the camera. Finn tapped a section of the screen. "But who's that shadowy figure in the back seat? It can't be Melanie, because she's in the passenger's seat."

Shay and Zoe didn't have an answer.

"I hope he trusts that person," Finn grumbled.

Zoe spoke up. "Bram trusts Tristan, aye? Then he would never allow anyone harmful to accompany him. Not to mention that no dragonman would ever put his own mate in danger. As long as Melanie is there, Tristan will be cautious."

His dragon chimed in. *You should've realized that yourself.*

Let's just say that I have other things on my mind.

Tristan engaged the speaker and his voice filled the guard station. "Tristan MacLeod and Melanie Hall-MacLeod, with a guest and a Protector."

Finn pressed the comm button. "Who is the guest?"

Tristan opened his mouth, but Melanie beat him to it. "George MacLeod."

Finn blinked. "Pardon?"

"George MacLeod, Tristan and Arabella's father," Melanie answered.

He tried to make out the male's features, but couldn't do so. "He's alive?"

Melanie bobbed her head. "Let us in and we'll explain it all. Brenna Rossi is here to watch over George full-time, to help ease your mind."

"You want me to let in someone who requires a full-time guard?" Finn demanded.

Melanie beat her mate to answering, "He only needs to be here long enough for Dr. MacFie to take a history and possibly a vial of blood."

"And why can't this be done back on Stonefire? Arabella doesn't need more stress."

Tristan spoke up. "I think Ara is finally ready for the truth, or I wouldn't be here."

His dragon chimed in. *If we turn him away, Ara may never forgive us.*

And if he's a threat? I shouldn't risk my family.

Between our Protectors and Stonefire's, we should be fine. You know Brenna's reputation. If she can manage the Irish clan's Protectors during an attack, she can handle watching one male.

Finn stared at the video feed for a few seconds. He finally sighed. "I'll allow you inside, but I want to talk with you lot first before I take you to Arabella."

Cutting off the microphone, Finn hit the gate release button and turned toward his two Protectors on duty. "Shay, let Faye and Grant know of the situation. You'll probably have to talk with them in person, at the surgery, since their phones might be muted. And Zoe, you'll be coming with me."

Used to following Finn's orders, Shay rushed out and Zoe followed Finn out of the building to the parked car outside.

Brenna Rossi's tall, dark-haired form emerged from the vehicle first.

With his initial shock gone, reason returned to Finn's brain. Considering Brenna had kept her mate sane through a recent ordeal, where the male had ended up with a two-headed inner dragon, she shouldn't have a problem keeping one dragon-shifter under control.

Melanie and Tristan disembarked next. While Finn wouldn't exactly say he was best friends with his brother-in-law, he respected Tristan's love and care for his human mate and twin bairns.

All three of them moved to stand together, just outside the car door that hadn't opened yet. Tristan glanced at Finn, and once he nodded, Tristan lifted the handle and pulled.

A male only slightly shorter than Finn, with gray hair and a well-worn face lined with frown and grimace lines, emerged. The car blocked most of his body, but the male walked in jerky movements. When he finally cleared the car, Finn saw why.

He used metal crutches that wrapped around his forearms and he gripped in his fists. Watching the material of his trousers move against his lower legs, Finn determined he had prosthetics.

Missing limbs still wasn't a reason to abandon a family. Finn would hear the truth, but he wasn't about to pity the male who should've helped Arabella when she'd needed it most.

Tristan motioned to his father. "George MacLeod, meet Finn Stewart, Lochguard's clan leader and Arabella's mate."

George studied Finn a second before the male averted his gaze to the side. Since George didn't say anything, Finn focused on Tristan. "I hope you have a bloody good reason for this, Tristan. I can't say that I'm at my most levelheaded at the moment. The male claiming to be your father abandoned Arabella, as well as you. What right does he have to be here now, when my family might be on the verge of a crisis?"

George murmured, "I have none."

Before Finn could do more than frown, Melanie jumped in. "A shouting match won't help Freya. Explanations can wait. It's more important that Dr. MacFie, Sid, and Gregor talk with George. Once that's done, then you two can have your shouting match."

"I didn't say I would shout," Finn pointed out. "But I'm not about to be charming."

Melanie rolled her eyes. "I'm not going to comment." She turned toward the main pathway. "Now, are you going to escort us to the surgery or should I just make my own way?"

With a grumble, Finn muttered, "Follow me." He pinned George with a stare, not caring that the male probably didn't see it because of his gaze remaining toward the ground. "Try anything, and I will toss you into a cell and allow the doctors to do their examinations that way."

George didn't answer. But Finn's dragon spoke up. *I think he's broken. Maybe ease up a wee bit on the threats.*

Until I know the truth, no, I won't. Arabella suffered be-

cause of him.

For all we know, that might not be entirely true. Besides, we can't change the past. And even if we could, doing so would probably result in us never finding Ara at all.

Not wanting to debate the point, Finn ignored his beast and picked up his pace. He took the rear entrance to the surgery and herded everyone into a private waiting room. He told one of the nurses to fetch a doctor before closing and locking the door. He looked at Tristan, Melanie, and George in turn. "I think whilst waiting for the doctor, you lot need to start talking and tell me what the bloody hell is going on."

Melanie didn't bat an eye at the dominance in his voice. "I understand that you're trying to protect Arabella, but you could try being less of an asshole."

Tristan snorted, but Finn ignored him. "I'll return to my charming self soon enough. However, my daughter's life and sanity could be in danger, not to mention Arabella's so-called father could send my mate back into a state of depression, or worse. You understand dragon-shifters almost better than any other human, Mel. So you know that until all threats are vanquished, I'm not going to ease up."

She sighed. "I know, but I keep thinking that someday I can talk some sense into one of you."

Tristan spoke up. "How about we just explain the situation?" He motioned toward George. "I only located him in the last year or so. I debated telling Ara, but then she found you and I didn't want to threaten her newfound happiness."

"Aye, well, it's been over a year. So start talking," Finn ordered.

George's quiet voice filled the space. "I went rogue shortly after my mate's death."

He zeroed in on the older male. Sensing George needed a second, Finn kept his mouth shut. George finally continued, "Finding out that your true mate was tortured and murdered, as well as the fact that your daughter was set on fire, isn't an easy thing to digest. I know dragon males are supposed to be strong and tackle any issue. But while I could pack away my grief and disgust at my own failure whilst Ara recovered from her burns, once she was released and back home, it crashed over me." He finally met Finn's gaze. The despair in the other male's eyes nearly made him suck in a breath. "My dragon thrashed about and took control. I barely made it into the air and to a remote part of Yorkshire before I lost any hold over my beast. I was fortunate to find a few clan-less dragon-shifters to keep me from doing something irreversible."

"You were gone over a decade," Finn pointed out.

"At first, I didn't fight my dragon. It was easier to let his instinct guide us than to dwell on my failures. However, when I teetered on the edge of destroying a local village, I resorted to drugs to keep my dragon silent."

"And you still never thought to contact your children?"

George shook his head. "Their lives were better without me."

"Coward," Finn growled.

"Yes, I was," George answered.

Finn's dragon spoke up. *He's clearly defeated. Whilst I detest his cowardice, yelling at him won't help Arabella or our children.*

But he abandoned *his family. That is unforgivable.*

I won't disagree. But it should be Arabella who decides whether to forgive him or push him away. Not us.

Finn grunted. "Rattling off my opinion of your actions is pointless, as they aren't the ones that matter. However, if Arabella tells you to leave Lochguard, you'll do so."

George nodded and Tristan chimed in. "George doesn't know the full extent of his allergies, but he mentioned something about having adverse reactions in the wild. I think it's best to let Sid or the other doctors do what they need to do before introducing him to Ara."

Finn noted how Tristan called his father by his given name, but decided to ask about it later. "Aye, I agree. You lot will stay here. I'm going to check on Ara and our bairns." He glanced at Brenna. "It's your duty to follow and enforce my order, aye?"

"I have no desire to cause trouble, Finn," Brenna answered.

"Right, then I'm off."

With that, Finn exited the room and ran a hand through his hair. *How am I going to break this to Arabella?*

Tell her the truth. That's all she wants.

You say that so easily, dragon.

Picking up his pace, Finn headed toward the nursery. His mate had no idea that her life was about to change yet again.

Maybe one day he could see through his promise to give her a safe, stable future.

Unfortunately, he wasn't there yet.

CHAPTER SIX

Since Faye had rushed out of the nursery on an urgent Protector matter, Arabella had put aside her laptop and rocked in the glider chair, ready in case one of her babies needed her. She usually tried to sleep when her children did, but even with her eyes closed, her brain kept whirling.

Her search hadn't yet brought up anything about her father, for one. And two, she wondered what was keeping Finn away for so long.

Her dragon spoke up. *He won't stay away longer than is absolutely necessary.*

I know, but for once, I actually want people around me. Is it wrong to wish for Aunt Lorna to come home as soon as possible? I miss her.

Of course it's not wrong. She is like a mother to us. Merely having her near will help both us and Freya.

She heard the door and instantly opened her eyes. Finn already stood at the crib, staring down at their children.

Standing, she crossed over to her mate. However, when he didn't pull her close and kiss her head, she knew something was wrong. Finn always did that after rushing off for an urgent matter, to let her know he'd missed her. "What happened?"

"Tristan and Melanie are here."

She frowned. "What? Why? Not that I don't want to see my brother and sister-in-law, but they weren't supposed to visit for weeks." With a sigh, Finn met her eyes. At his unreadable expression, her heart skipped a beat and every worst-case scenario ran through her head. "Please tell me that they're okay and the twins are, too."

"They're all fine."

At his monotone answer, irritation flared. Mindful of the babies, she kept her tone low, but firm. "Just tell me what's going on, Finn. You hesitating is only making the situation worse."

Gently taking hold of her bicep, he guided her to the far side of the room before whispering, "Tristan found your father."

Her heart skipped a beat. "That's impossible."

Finn shook his head. "No, he's here. Dr. Sid and Gregor should be with him as we speak."

She was torn between wanting to rush out of the room to find her father and staying put to avoid him.

Her dragon grunted. *We shouldn't cower in this situation. You wanted closure. This would be it.*

I need more information before I rush to him. We have no idea what he's been up to.

Meeting Finn's gaze, she asked, "Something must be off. Otherwise, you wouldn't be so quiet and restrained."

He sighed. "You know me too well, love."

Placing a hand on his chest, she leaned closer to murmur, "Just tell me, Finn."

He wrapped his arms around her and pulled her against his body. "He's here, but I suspect different than you remember. It's almost as if he's given up, and you never mentioned that about him before."

More than anyone, Arabella understood feeling defeated. If she hadn't met Finn, she might've given up, too. "Do you know where he's been?"

Finn rubbed slow circles on her back. "In hiding." Finn relayed what he knew of her father's hiding and subsequent drug dependency before adding, "Tell me what to do, Ara. If you want him gone, I'll order it. If you want to meet him, I'll arrange that too. But I hope you understand why I met him alone first, before you could."

She nodded. "I do. If you hadn't told me about him, then I'd be bloody upset and shouting when I found out. But you did tell me. And now I can face him without shock clouding my brain."

He kissed her forehead. "My brilliant mate never ceases to amaze me."

Normally, she'd make a quip, but Arabella was exhausted, and it looked as if she need to reserve what strength she did have. "When can I see him?"

Leaning back, he cupped her cheek. "Until I'm positive he's not a threat, I won't allow him near our children. That means leaving them for a short while under someone else's care because I'm going with you."

"I know." She traced Finn's jaw with a finger. Just as she tried to decide who would be the best choice to watch over her babies, the door opened to reveal Aunt Lorna's gray and blonde-haired, slightly plump form.

Lorna rushed over to them. "I came back as soon as I could." She hugged the pair of them. "Is it true? What Faye told me about Freya?"

Arabella answered first. "Yes. She's stable for now, although the doctors are working on a more long-term solution." She looked behind Lorna, but didn't see her mate. "Is Ross with Holly?"

"Aye. Holly's getting closer to giving birth, which means Fraser is driving her crazy. So Ross is acting as peacekeeper."

Despite everything going on, Arabella couldn't help but smile. "Is that wise? Usually, there's only more fighting whenever Ross and Fraser get together."

Lorna clicked her tongue. "Both of them are to be on their best behaviors, as they promised me. But that lot will be fine. Tell me what I can do to help my granddaughter."

Something as simple as Lorna thinking of Freya as her granddaughter instead of great-niece helped Arabella relax a fraction. The one thing that the MacKenzies always had in ample supply was love.

Well, and stubbornness. But their love was more important.

Arabella moved to the crib, and Finn and Aunt Lorna followed. Arabella kept her gaze on the three sleeping babies. "I know you just returned, but could you watch Freya and the boys for a short while? Finn and I have something to do."

Lorna looked at the pair. "I sense it's important, but that you don't want to discuss it right now. As long as you promise to do so when possible, then aye, it's not a hardship to watch the triplets. They're angels compared to when my own children were their age."

"I think you're lying about that, Aunt Lorna. But we can talk about that later." Arabella hugged the older dragon-woman. "Thank you." Releasing her, Arabella glanced at Finn. "Let's go."

He raised an eyebrow. "Are you sure you want to do this now?"

"Yes." Taking Finn's hand, she squeezed it. "I stopped running and hiding when I met you, and I bloody well won't start doing it again now."

Raising their clasped hands, Finn kissed the back of hers. "I love you, Arabella. You're so bloody brilliant."

She resisted blushing. Arabella still had trouble with compliments, no matter how many times Finn gave them. "Some of your grumpiness has faded, which is a good sign. Let's hope it stays that way for this meeting."

He nodded at his aunt, and they exited the room. "I can't promise anything with regards to my grumpiness. But let me know if you need to leave. We could devise a code, or you could simply tell me you want to go."

"Normally, I'd create the worst code word I could think of, but I'm exhausted, worried about Freya, and nervous about meeting my dad." She threaded her arm through his. "Just having you near will be a great help."

After kissing the top of her head, they walked the rest of the way in a comfortable silence. Finn at her side gave her the extra bit of courage she'd need for what was to come.

She couldn't imagine her life without him.

Her dragon spoke up. *Don't forget about me. I'm here to help, too. Always.*

Pushing aside the guilt that flared at the decade Arabella had all but ignored her inner beast, she replied, *And I'll never take that for granted again, love. I promise.*

Finn finally stopped them in front of a door to a private room. "He's in here."

Taking a deep breath, Arabella opened the door.

A gray-haired male with slumped shoulders sat with his back to her. While he'd always sat tall when she'd been a child, she recognized the form of her father.

Tristan was across the room, with Melanie at her side. Tristan spoke before she could say anything. "Arabella."

She waited for her father to turn his head, but George MacLeod kept his gaze on the ground in front of him.

Despite her rational intentions, she gripped Finn's hand tightly to avoid screaming at her dad. When he'd been at her bedside, during her recovery from the severe burns she'd received from the dragon hunters setting half her body on fire, she'd taken comfort from his strong hand gripping her non-burned one, his gentle voice persuading her to fight.

It had only been when he'd vanished that she'd realized how much her father had kept her grounded and fighting during that critical period of her life.

And now he wouldn't even look at her.

Emotion choked her throat.

Her brother repeated, "Arabella."

At her usually gruff brother's soft voice, she finally looked up. Part of her wanted to run to him. Finn was her mate and she loved him, but Tristan had been the one to fight for her when she'd been younger, in place of her father.

And she'd missed him.

As if reading her thoughts, Tristan closed the distance between them and opened his arms. Without a word, Finn released her hand and Tristan hugged her close. He murmured, "I'm sorry I didn't tell you earlier."

Shaking her head against her brother's chest, she replied, "No, it's okay. I just missed you."

Tristan grunted. "With the twins being older, I'm sure we can visit more often." He leaned back and touched her chin. "Just tell us what you want to do right now and I'm sure we'll all follow it."

She glanced at Finn and he nodded his agreement.

The easiest path would be to say she wanted to leave, go back to her children, and forget about the male who'd abandoned her as a teenager.

And yet, to do so would erase much of the progress she'd made over the last few years.

She'd promised herself that she wouldn't run again, and Arabella was determined to fulfill that vow.

Taking a deep breath, she pushed away from Tristan and took a few steps toward her father.

Standing just behind her dad, she noticed the metal crutches lying next to him. Since he hadn't needed them before, something must've happened to him too.

Despite everything, she wanted to know what.

Mustering her courage, Arabella moved to stand in front of her father. Since he still didn't look up, she spoke. "Dad, look at me."

One beat passed and then another. Just as she debated squatting to see his face, George MacLeod met her gaze.

The guilt and self-hatred in his brown eyes were more than familiar. Arabella had seen it in the mirror every day for years.

She might still be angry and wouldn't forgive him without a lot more discussion and time, but in that moment, she knew she wanted to help him.

Because she sensed that if she didn't, he might not live much longer. And despite everything that had happened, her children deserved to have another grandparent.

Not just because her father's genetics might better help understand what was going on with Freya, but because somewhere deep inside the self-loathing male in front of her was the male she remembered. The one with pieces of her and Tristan's quirks and personalities.

On top of that, he was one of the few links to her mother.

Crouching down, she took her father's hands in hers. He tried to pull them away, but she tightened her grip. "No, I'm not going to let you hide and run away any longer." His gaze shot to the healed burns on her neck. She growled. "Yes, I suffered when I was younger. And of course, I missed my father and wished he would've been around to help. But right now, you're the one who needs support, and I'm going to give it to you."

She barely heard his words, "I'm not worth it."

"Stop. Because if you keep it up, I'll call in a female here by the name of Aunt Lorna. And I assure you, she's a much stronger force to be reckoned with than me. But one way or the other, I'm going to help you, Father. You have five grandchildren so far, and they deserve to know the male I remember, not this half-shadow you've become."

She held her breath and waited. From her own experience, Arabella knew that sometimes a person needed a little time to voice a thought, or even accept someone's offer of help.

The others in the room must've sensed the same, because they remained silent, too.

Her father finally spoke again. "I abandoned you and Tristan, Ara. You should be angry with me."

She raised an eyebrow. "I am, but we can deal with that later, once you stop hating yourself. Because I was once just like you. It took a lot of love from Tristan and his mate, as well as finding my own true mate, to finally move past it. The experience taught me that love can heal many wounds, including the ones you have now." She squeezed his hands in hers. "But I also know that it won't make any sort of difference unless you want to live."

Arabella released her dad's hands and took out her mobile. After finding a picture of her three babies sleeping together, she turned it toward them. "Here are three reasons you should fight, Dad. These are my three babies—Freya, Grayson, and Declan." She changed to another picture of two toddlers. "And here are two more. These are Tristan's twins, Jack and Annabel." Lowering the phone, she whispered, "So the most important question is—do you want to fight for the chance to know your grandbabies? Or do you want to give up, and abandon all of us again?"

Her father's gaze moved to Tristan. "Do you agree with Ara?"

Tristan grunted. "Yes. I've been trying to tell you that for months, but you never listened. However, know that if you walk away this time, I won't follow. This is it, George. Either allow us to help you heal, or you'll never see or hear from us again."

Her brother's words were harsher than Arabella's, but it was Tristan's way. If her father wanted to stay in their lives, he'd have to learn to accept both of them as they were in the present.

Looking back at Arabella, her dad murmured, "Can I see their pictures again?"

She unlocked the phone and found one of the few photos with all the children together and handed it to him.

A minute or more passed before he whispered, "Jocelyn would've loved to spoil them all."

Pushing past the sadness at her mum's absence, she pointed to Freya. "My daughter's full name is Freya Anne Jocelyn Stewart. Finn's mother was killed, too, like Mum. So I thought our daughter should have both of her grandmothers' names as part of her own, to remember where she came from."

A tear rolled down her father's face. He quickly wiped it away and met her gaze. "I want to know them, Ara. If you'll let me."

Emotion choked her throat. Rather than tell him how she felt with words, she hugged her father. It took a second for him to hug her back.

In that moment, the years apart didn't matter. Her father's hug and warm presence were a comfort she thought she'd never have again.

There may be a lot of work to do, but she was happy to have her dad back again. The question was whether he'd keep up the fight or not.

When she finally released her dad, she turned toward Finn and asked with her eyes if they could show him their triplets. Finn nodded, moved to pick up her dad's crutches, and held them out. "Aye, well, you'll be staying here for the foreseeable future. You and I will have our own chat later. But for now, I think we should introduce you to our bairns as well as Aunt Lorna." As her dad took his crutches and stood, Finn added, "But just know that if you do anything to upset my family, you'll deal with me."

Her father nodded, but remained silent. Arabella chimed in. "Right, then let's go." She looked at Tristan and Melanie. "You two should come, too. I know you'll have to return to Stonefire soon enough, but hopefully, you can at least spend the night."

Melanie smiled. "Since the DDA granted my parents a few weeks' leave to stay on Stonefire, they're watching the twins. I'm sure Jack and Annabel will be spoiled enough to forget they even have parents for a few days."

Humans that weren't mated to a dragon-shifter had to possess a special pass from the UK Home Office before they could stay on a clan's land. Melanie had been instrumental in convincing the Home Office to issue more passes, especially for family members.

"Good," Arabella stated. "Then you can spend a day or two with the triplets. As it is, we have a lot going on right now. And I'll admit, we could use all the help we can get."

Melanie didn't miss a beat. "Ask anytime for our help and we'll give it. You know that, Ara."

Arabella owed much of her recovery to her sister-in-law, both with Melanie's influence on Tristan as well as the Department of Dragon Affairs. Without her sister-in-law's book on dragon-shifters, Bram and Finn may never have reached a foster candidate agreement. Meaning Arabella never would've found and mated Finn.

Yes, she was going to work on seeing her family on Stonefire more often, if she could manage it.

As they all filed out of the room, Arabella waved hello to Brenna Rossi, who had been standing guard, and then kept pace with her father's slower one. She had so many questions, but most of them would have to wait. Not just because of Freya, but also because she wanted to ensure Holly survived the delivery of her twins without a hitch. All signs pointed to routine births, but Arabella never dismissed outliers.

Especially since if anything happened to Holly, she had no idea how her true mate, Fraser, would react.

Her dragon spoke up. *Don't think like that. Holly will be fine.*

Rather than argue, she merely took the time to steal glances at her dad. He had more wrinkles than before, and grayer hair.

But he was still her father. Him meeting her children was hopefully the first step on his long recovery, both with himself and her family

~

Finn watched Arabella as she walked alongside her father. He would normally have Fergus reach out to his contacts to find out everything he could about George MacLeod. However, with his cousin in the throes of a mate-claim frenzy, Finn had asked one of the other Protectors, Brodie, to do so.

His dragon spoke up. *You trust Brodie, too.*

I know, but this is extremely important. I want to trust Ara's father, but for all we know, he could secretly be working for the rogue dragon-shifters.

Not long after Finn had won control of the clan, a group of disgruntled clan members had put his mate in danger. As a result, he'd exiled them and any others who didn't want to follow his leadership. The rogue pack of dragon-shifters now hid in the wilds somewhere in Scotland, planning who knew what. They had already troubled his family before, when they'd kidnapped Holly. Ever since, he'd vowed that he would do whatever it took to disband them and ensure they received justice for their crimes.

His dragon said, *But we have a plan in place. Soon, we'll have a spy inside their ranks.*

He and Bram had a long-term strategy, which they could finally enact in the coming months. *Aye, I know, but it's not soon enough.*

Arabella paused at the door to the nursery and glanced at him. Once he nodded, she entered, her father at her side, Finn and the others close on her heels.

Inside, Aunt Lorna had wee Freya in her arms as she rocked the glider chair. Since Freya loved her honorary grandmother nearly as much as her parents, she slept peacefully in Aunt Lorna's arms. Lorna's low voice filled the room. "Just be careful to keep your voices down, aye? I just got her back to sleep."

Arabella gestured toward her father. "Lorna MacKenzie Anderson, may I present my father, George MacLeod."

Lorna took in Arabella's father. To most, her smile would seem friendly and nothing else. But Finn saw the assessing nature of her gaze, which was quickly replaced with a neutral expression. "Hello, George. I must say, it's hard to believe you're standing here."

"Aunt Lorna," Arabella warned.

The older dragonwoman raised her brows. "I only speak the truth. After all, as long as my children are alive, I won't be far away. I couldn't imagine abandoning them."

Arabella opened her mouth, but George beat her to it. "She's right, Ara."

"Aye, I usually am." Lorna scrutinized George. "But you

being here now, when you learned that your granddaughter needed help, speaks volumes. I'll give you one chance, George MacLeod. But hurt anyone I hold dear, and I'll ensure you leave shortly thereafter."

Finn resisted a sigh. Anyone who thought alpha male dragons were overly protective had clearly never met Aunt Lorna; females could be just as bad. "He's been warned already, Auntie. How about we try to avoid issuing threats for at least an hour? This is the first time he's meeting any of his grandchildren, after all."

Lorna cuddled Freya tighter against her body. "This wee lass is staying right here. I don't want to risk her dragon coming out." She motioned toward the crib with the boys. "But the lads have been stirring and probably wish to wake up."

Arabella guided her father to the crib, but Finn moved closer to his aunt. After lightly running a finger down his daughter's soft cheek, he murmured, "Tone down the threats, Aunt Lorna. Ara wants to help him."

"Aye, well, I seem to recall honesty being the way you won the lass. It can't hurt to try it with her father."

He did sigh at that and decided to change the subject. "What happened to Faye and Grant?"

"They went to check on Holly. Apparently, Ross and Fraser are having a wee row."

"I'm surprised you didn't see that coming, considering how well you know the family."

His aunt huffed. "I expected better, considering Holly's in labor. Although given my youngest son's way, he may have orchestrated it all to distract Holly from the pain."

"Aye, that's possible. Although I think you're giving him too much credit."

"Fraser is about to become a father. I believe there are many things he doesn't even know about himself, but will show up soon enough."

"We'll see." Finn took out his mobile and quickly checked his text messages, but there wasn't anything from his family members.

After one more quick look to ensure his daughter was asleep, he moved closer to Arabella and her father. George now sat in one of the chairs, and Arabella settled their more social son, Declan, into his arms.

At the sight of George looking down at wee Declan with awe in his eyes, Finn wanted to believe everything would be all right. More than anyone, Arabella deserved greater happiness in her life.

Hopefully his Protectors would find nothing on George. But he'd just have to wait and see.

Chapter Seven

Fraser MacKenzie took a step toward his father-in-law. "Holly wanted a completely natural birth without any drugs, so as to not interfere with the results of her dragon's blood shots. I'm merely honoring her request."

Ross Anderson narrowed his eyes and waved toward Holly. "She's in pain, Fraser. The window has nearly passed for her to have anything, even the tamer dragon-shifter-safe ones."

"Holly isn't a child. She can make her own decisions."

Fraser moved closer to his father-in-law when Holly's tired, yet firm voice rang out. "Stop it, the both of you. And come here."

His dragon spoke up. *She may not be a dragon-shifter, but I often forget she can thread dominance into her voice like a clan leader.*

Ignoring his beast, he rushed to Holly's side and took her hand. "Do I need to fetch the doctor, honey? Is it time?"

"You two need to stop fighting." Holly switched her gaze to her father. "I'm an adult and can make my own decisions, Dad. A little pain means nothing if it can help save the lives of thousands of other humans mated to dragon-shifters around the world."

Fraser kissed her brow. "That's my female, always thinking of others before herself." He laid his forehead against hers. "Just promise me that if things turn south, you do what's best for you, regardless of how it affects the experiment."

Before she could answer, she closed her eyes and sucked in a breath.

Another contraction had hit.

He murmured soothing words until it passed. Holly opened her eyes, and he wished he could erase the pain in her golden-brown eyes. Her voice was faint as she said, "Call the doctor. I think we're getting close."

Before Fraser could do anything, Ross rushed to the call button and then raced out of the room to probably find someone just in case. He and the human male might have their differences of opinion, but Fraser would've done the same thing.

He's also quick for his age, his beast added.

"Fraser." He focused back on his mate, and she added, "Be nice to Dad. He's merely worried. I'm his only child, after all."

"I know, honey. But acting normal with your dad helps to calm me down and not think about the worst-case scenario. I don't want to lose you."

Raising a hand, she cupped his cheek. "I'll be fine, Fraser. I know what it's like to grow up most of my life without a mother and I'll be damned if I'll let that happen to my children."

He kissed her. "Good. Because I like having you around, too. It'd be an absolute madhouse at dinner without you there."

She pinched his cheek and he flinched. "Good to see I'm only useful to bring truces to you and your sister."

"Don't say that, honey. I love you." He kissed her slowly. "I don't want to ever imagine my life without you."

"Oh, Fraser."

She sucked in another breath and gripped his hand tighter. By his count, the contractions were coming fairly close together.

He debated going to find a doctor himself when Dr. Layla MacFie rushed in, tugging on her second glove. Before he could ask what had taken so long, Layla spoke. "Right, then let's check and see how dilated you are, Holly. It's not every day I have a midwife in labor, but I imagine it feels a bit differently from the other side of the coin, no?" Layla placed her hand between Holly's thighs and then nodded. "Aye, it should be any time now. Let's get you situated." She glanced at Ross. "And I want you to wait outside. One alpha male is enough for me to handle during a delivery."

Ross rushed to Holly's other side and kissed her cheek. "I won't be far, Holly-berry. Shout for me and I'll come running at full speed."

"I'd like to see you try running that fast. Maybe you could set a time record on Lochguard," Holly said, humor dancing in her eyes.

"Cheeky lass." Ross touched his daughter's face one last time before exiting the room.

Never taking his eyes from Holly, Fraser asked, "What should I do, Layla?"

"Stay out of my way and support your mate. I'll give you one warning before I kick you out, too."

He met the doctor's gaze then. "I'm not going anywhere."

Layla shrugged. "Then behave and we won't have a problem."

A good dragon-shifter doctor needed to be able to put any dragon in his place, alpha or not. Seeing as Holly wasn't the first female to give birth today, Layla had probably perfected her technique earlier with Hamish Boyd.

Holly tensed again, and Layla went into motion. "Since

Sid and Gregor had to help with another patient and are now on call, Logan should be coming soon, so let's get you up."

Fraser helped Holly sit up as the doctor placed her legs into the stirrups.

As the minutes ticked by and Holly rode out the contractions, Fraser murmured soothing words about his bonny lass.

But deep down, he worried. A normal human female's chances at birthing a dragon-shifter child was fifty-fifty. Holly's hypothesis was that injections of dragon's blood increased a human female's chances of survival.

Increasing her chances wasn't enough, though. He wanted a guarantee.

His dragon said, *She will be fine. Believe in our mate.*

I'm trying.

Finally, Layla looked to each of them in turn. "It's time. When the next contraction comes, push for me, Holly."

The recently arrived nurse, Logan, stood to the side waiting. Fraser wanted to shout for him to do something.

His dragon sighed. *Logan is one of the best nurses on Lochguard. He wouldn't be standing still if there was anything else that needed to be done right this second.*

Holly gripped his hand so hard it felt as if she'd break his bones, and every other thought fled his mind. His mate needed him.

Never taking her gaze from her task, Layla said, "There's the first head. You're doing brilliantly, Holly. Keep it up."

Some females might curse and lash out, but his brave, strong lass merely went through the next few contractions like a champ, pushing when asked and stopping when needed.

Eventually, a small cry filled the room and Layla held up a tiny, red-haired bairn. "You have a daughter."

Since dragon-shifters waited until the birth to find out the genders, Fraser murmured, "A daughter." He kissed Holly's forehead. "A daughter, honey."

"A ginger-haired MacKenzie menace, I'm sure," she murmured with love in her voice.

Even when exhausted and in pain, his love found a way to tease.

Layla handed his daughter off to Logan. "I want to get both of them delivered, and then you can hold them. We'll take a short break and then try again, aye?"

As he watched Logan tend to the wee bairn, it finally hit Fraser that he was now a dad.

And all he could think about was everything that could go wrong or harm his daughter.

His dragon huffed. *Logan won't hurt her.*

Holly's weak voice garnered his attention. "Fraser, help me with the next one, aye? I've been exhausted before, but this is a new level. I need your strength, and then you can glower at anyone who looks at our daughter."

His strong mate rarely asked for help, which meant she needed it.

He kissed the back of her hand. "I'm here for you, honey. Always."

She smiled. "I love you."

Layla's voice interrupted his reply. "The second bairn is behaving and is in position. With any luck, he or she will take after Holly's temperament and not make a scene coming into the world."

Fraser growled, but Holly squeezed his hand. "Not now, Fraser."

He somehow managed to murmur support and kiss his mate until Layla said, "Right, then let's try again."

Holly repeated her silent, brave performance, barely murmuring a peep of pain during the process.

But deep down, he knew it had to be painful. He'd just have to pamper her for as long as she wanted, even if it were for years, to make up for childbirth.

Soon, a second small cry filled the room, and Layla grinned as she held up another red-haired lass. "Twin daughters. I almost think it's a punishment of sorts, for what you and Fergus put your mum through, Fraser."

"Two daughters," he echoed.

"Identical I'd say, at first glance." She waited for Logan to clip the umbilical cord before taking her over to the infant check station. "Logan, take the first bairn to meet her parents, and I'll check this one."

Fraser laid his cheek against Holly's, never taking his gaze from the wee bundle in Logan's arms. He came and placed their daughter in Holly's arms.

The wee, wrinkled face was one of the most beautiful things he'd ever seen.

His dragon huffed. *She's like a hairless rat.*

Shut it, dragon.

He kissed his daughter's forehead and then kissed Holly's lips. "We have two daughters, honey."

Despite her exhaustion, Holly smiled. "Which is rare for dragon-shifters, from what I've heard."

"Aye, it is. But also a sign of good luck. Everyone will tell you so."

As he stared at their first daughter's face, he couldn't help but wonder for a second if the bairn they'd lost would've been a female as well.

No. He pushed the thought aside. He'd never forget their first bairn, but right now, his two living ones needed him.

Logan brought their second daughter and placed her in Holly's other arm, with Fraser supporting her. He also kissed the other lass's forehead.

As he leaned against his mate and stared at his two

daughters, happiness flooded his body. He would do whatever it took to protect them and give them the loving family he'd had growing up.

Holly's tired voice filled his ear. "Well, with two lasses, I suppose that means I'll have to allow one of your name choices, too. Just avoid Agnes, if you could."

"But wee Aggie would be such a bonny name."

"Aye, until they start calling her Haggie Aggie, or some other such thing."

He smiled. "You have a point. But you name one first and I'll do the other."

Holly looked at their firstborn. "Then Skye MacKenzie it is."

Skye was an island in Scotland. "Being named for one of the most beautiful places in Scotland isn't too bad." Fraser looked at their second-born. All of the names he'd pitched previously fled his mind. He wanted to honor the tradition his mother had done, giving both of his children names beginning with the same letter.

Then the perfect name came to him. "Summer MacKenzie it is. Because when you put summer and Skye together, there's no place as bonny or breathtaking. For beauty, aye, but also full of surprises and adventure, which I'm sure this pair will have plenty of."

Holly nodded. "I love it. Hello, Summer and Skye. Try not to cause too much trouble for your mum and dad."

Fraser grinned. "You are aware they're half MacKenzie, aye? We may as well make Trouble and Mischief their middles names."

"Then let them save it for their aunts and uncles. It may be a pointless task, but I'd like a bit less chaos in our own house than in your mum's."

"I doubt that's possible, but you'll find that out soon enough."

Holly stuck out her tongue and he chuckled.

Cuddling his mate and two daughters, Fraser couldn't think of any other place he'd rather be. Happy wasn't enough to describe how he felt. He had so much love for his daughters after mere moments, it was hard to believe it.

But one thing was certain—anyone or thing that tried to harm his family would have to deal with him. Fraser wasn't a warrior, but a father's love changed a male.

And with Holly at his side, he could tackle anything.

Chapter Eight

Arabella watched her father as he played with Grayson. Her dad's eyes were full of happiness, and it was as if his self-hating persona disappeared when he had one of his grandchildren in his arms.

Her dragon spoke up. *Then he should stay with us.*

I'm not sure if Finn would like that.

You can at least ask him.

Arabella looked to her side, where Finn stood. She opened her mouth, but Ross rushed into the room and shouted, "I have two granddaughters!"

She blinked. "They had two females? I've never personally known any dragon-shifter to have twin females before."

Ross puffed his chest. "Aye, the nurse told me it's a sign of good luck. It must be my excellent genes."

Lorna rolled her eyes, but couldn't fight off a smile. "Mine played a part as well, you daft fool."

Ross gave Lorna a quick kiss. "You had twin boys, as did Finn and Ara. That's your side's genetics. The good old Anderson stock brought the luck."

Finn sighed. "Can you two argue about that later? When can we see them?"

"Dr. MacFie says soon, once she's delivered the afterbirth."

As Ross murmured with his mate, Arabella whispered to Finn, "You do realize that those poor babies are going to have an impossible time. Not only because everyone will tell them their whole lives that they're good luck and will bring an era of peace, but Fraser as an overprotective father is going to test everyone's patience."

Finn grunted. "I suspect so. But if the old tale of twin female dragon-shifters bringing peace between dragons and humans is even a wee bit true, Fraser's antics will pale by comparison. I'll sort him out somehow."

She raised her brows. "Oh? Do you have a new technique I'm unaware of?"

He squeezed her waist. "Aye, if he doesn't behave then I'll tell the clan that visiting his daughters weekly will help usher in good luck to their families."

"That isn't part of the old legends," she drawled.

"So? Everyone will assume it's from a version they haven't heard."

She shook her head. "And that will rein him in, how? Fraser isn't a hermit. He enjoys socializing."

"Socializing, yes, but would you want Meg Boyd and her beaus in your house on a weekly basis, telling you how to raise the bairns properly?'

She snorted. "Fair point." Her gaze trailed to her father, who sat with a sleeping Grayson in his arms. Maybe she should wait until later, but she hated not knowing. So, she blurted, "Finn, I think my father should live with us."

For a few seconds, her mate remained silent. She started to wonder if he would outright deny her.

When he finally replied, she could barely hear it. "Maybe. Once I have my background check, I can let you know." Her face must've given away her feelings, because Finn added, "I know you want to help him, love. And while my surname may be Stewart, I was mostly raised a MacKenzie and you know we don't turn away those who need help. But I need to ensure he's not a threat first."

A different female may have pouted or tried to convince their mate they were wrong just because. But that wasn't Arabella's way. "I want to say no, I don't understand your way of thinking. And yet, I do. Just promise me that you'll tell me what you find as soon as possible. He's been so happy with the boys, and with a little work, I think he can be that way most of the time."

He nodded. "I have faith that he can be someday, too. But I want a promise from you too, aye? Don't forget about your own feelings and unresolved anger. When the time is right, you need to talk to him about it."

"I will." Finn raised his brows, unconvinced, and she added, "I promise that I'll talk to him. Because for as long as I put it off, I give you free rein to badger me about it. And the less of that I have to endure, the better."

He grinned. "Then I'll just have to make the most of it whilst I can."

She nearly groaned, but Freya stirred in her crib, garnering her attention. Arabella rushed to her daughter and sighed in relief when she saw her pupils were round. "We'll have you home in no time, Freya, love. Just cooperate a little longer for Mummy and Daddy, okay?"

Her daughter drooled.

Chuckling, Arabella picked up her daughter and carried her to where George sat. "And this is your granddad, Freya. He's spoiling your brother at the moment, but he'll be doing the same with you soon enough."

Her father met her eyes at that, filled with surprise. She added, "Dr. Sid should have her blood test results soon since she's conducting them herself. I'm hoping for it to be an allergy. If so, there's no reason you shouldn't have a chance to hold your youngest granddaughter."

After nodding, her dad looked back at sleeping Grayson and smiled.

Maybe everything would end up being all right with her family after all.

Family. A few years ago, she never would've hoped for such a thing.

Her dragon spoke up. *Which means we shouldn't take it for granted.*

Of course not.

Focusing on the people in the room instead of her dragon, Arabella said, "Right, then let's get everyone changed and fed so that when Layla gives the word, we can visit Fraser, Holly, and their twins."

Melanie, Tristan, and Finn all rushed to her side and helped. While it would be nice to have so much help every day, Arabella enjoyed the closeness of some alone time with her children.

Because she had a feeling that once they and their cousins were older, she would rarely be alone with her triplets. Not that it was a bad thing—Arabella wished that she'd had the same when she'd been younger—but she would treasure the little moments while she still could.

Finn had lost the battle to carry one of his own children to Fraser and Holly's room, so he followed his mate, Tristan, and Melanie, each of them with a bairn in tow.

Arabella's father had elected to stay in a hospital room, with Brenna watching over him. Since a breeze could've blown over the male, Finn hadn't fought it. Maybe George would even have his first peaceful sleep in years.

His dragon spoke up. *So now you're being overly forgiving.*

It's temporary. If I find anything that smells of betrayal or treason, I won't hesitate to change tactics. However, I doubt allowing him a nap will destroy the clan.

They finally reached the correct room. Aunt Lorna was the first to enter, with Ross at her side. Finn and the rest followed suit.

Fraser sat next to Holly on her bed, each of them holding a yellow-swaddled bundle. Fraser was family, so Finn blurted out, "And the shenanigans have begun. You could've put them in different colors so we could better keep track of which one is which."

Grinning, Fraser met his gaze. "We can tell them apart, so you should be able to as well."

Holly muttered, "Don't listen to him. The oldest, Skye, has an ink mark on her right hand."

Aunt Lorna clicked her tongue. "Finn knows that because of his own lads. Now, how about you introduce us? I'm anxious to hold my new grandbabies."

Fraser pointed to one and then the other as he said, "This here is Skye, and this is Summer."

"Such lovely names," Melanie said from the side of the room, where she gently jostled Grayson.

Finn looked down at the wee red faces. "They're so tiny."

Lorna answered as she picked up Skye. "They're early, so of course they're wee." She kissed Skye's cheek. "Gran will always have your back, little one. Remember that for the future, when your dad tries to protect you by locking you in your rooms. I might be able to help you escape for a little adventure, or argue for your freedom."

Ross took Summer into his arms. "Which means you two can run to granddad and I'll spoil you rotten when your father isn't looking."

"Just don't indulge them too much, Dad," Holly said with a smile.

“Has Fraser explained the significance of having twin females to you yet, Holly?” Arabella asked.

Holly moved her gaze to Arabella. “Aye, although I had no idea twin female dragon-shifters were rare. I just thought that Lochguard and Stonefire produced a lot of lads.”

“Well, dragon-shifters skew male in the first place,” Melanie chimed in. “Otherwise the DDA would never have agreed to the sacrifice program, and neither one of us would be here, Holly.”

Both Melanie and Holly had volunteered to be sacrifices to the dragon-shifter clans in exchange for a vial of dragon’s blood. Melanie had used it to heal her brother, and Holly had sold hers so that she could pay for her dad’s experimental cancer treatment.

Holly sat up a little bit more. “Then maybe someone could explain the finer details of it all? I know they’re meant to bring peace, but I haven’t had a chance to ask for more than that.”

Finn spoke up. “Aye, well, it’s related to stories about Alviva, Queen of the British dragon-shifters shortly after the Roman conquest of Britain. Almost every dragon-shifter knows that she forged an agreement with the Romans for fair treatment and semi-autonomy. But she didn’t do it alone. People tend to forget it was her and her twin sister, Edwina, who secured the deal.”

Lorna chimed in. “Aye, and while the details have been lost to history, the peace brought on by two females was put down to them being identical twins. Even though it was their skill and cleverness that did it, the males needed a reason to justify as to why so-called weak females could be so successful.”

Finn stepped in. “Regardless, it’s happened a few more times throughout history. The sacrifice program, to ensure our species’ survival, was also negotiated by twin females.

And there are rumors about another pair here and there, although I'm sure Alistair Boyd could tell you more about it than I ever could."

Finn had known Alistair Boyd his whole life, and the male taught history to young dragon-shifters.

Holly frowned. "Don't take this the wrong way, but I'm not going to force a future on my daughters. So if there's an expectation that I have to train them to be saviors, or what have you, I'm not going to do it."

Fraser answered, "There's no savior training, honey. But people will comment on it often, so it's better to prepare our daughters for the talk rather than to have others foist some fictional destiny on them."

Melanie spoke up from the side of the room. "I don't believe in fictional destinies, but maybe they will help in some way. If it's happened several times throughout history, it's bound to happen again. Who knows, maybe they can finally secure peace between all dragon-shifters and maybe even with the humans."

Finn sighed. "You never think small, do you, Mel?"

Melanie grinned. "If I did, I wouldn't be standing here right now."

Lorna cleared her throat. "How about we save talk of influence and destiny for later? The lasses are barely an hour old. Maybe they can learn to walk and talk first, aye?"

Finn held out his arms and Lorna placed Skye into them. As he readjusted the blanket around the bairn's sleeping face, he said, "I agree. But at least Freya will have some female cousins to play with."

"You mean plan to take over the world with."

At his cousin Faye's voice, he glanced at the door. "It's not nice to sneak up on someone holding a sleeping bairn."

Faye rolled her eyes. "I wasn't sneaking, just walking." She walked over to Ross, who transferred Summer into her arms. "I wanted to say hello to my latest recruits. Auntie Faye is going to ensure all her nieces can take care of themselves, when needed."

Holly bobbed her head. "I like that idea."

Fraser added, "As long as it doesn't involve you putting them into dangerous situations, then maybe I'll allow it."

"Allow it? Brother, you won't have a say in it."

Fraser raised his brows. "Does that mean I get to advise your bairns on how to get into mischief? That's only fair."

"Mischief is not the same as self-defense training," Faye said softly, so as to not disturb the bairns. "Besides, you may be out of luck, anyway. They may both take after Grant."

Ross snorted. "I somehow think that may not be in your cards, Faye, my dear. That would be too easy."

Fraser grunted. "For once, I agree with Ross."

As Faye and Fraser continued to argue about influencing each other's children—albeit in soothing, quiet tones—Finn noticed Grant in the doorway, bouncing wee Jamie. He shared a looked with the Protector; Grant signaled that he had finished the background check on George MacLeod.

After kissing Skye's forehead, Finn waited for Aunt Lorna to take Freya before handing over the bairn to Arabella. He whispered, "I'll be right back, love."

Arabella nodded, and Finn went into the hallway. Once he closed the door, he demanded, "Well?"

Grant didn't miss a beat. "For the most part, he's clean. Although he's been receiving hospital care in Perth, which is less than forty miles from where some of the rogue dragon-shifters have been spotted in Cairngorms National Park."

George's former location didn't automatically make the male guilty. Finn would have to check into it more soon. "Did you find out where he's been living?"

"In an abandoned cottage, somewhere in the countryside

between Perth and Cairngorms National Park. He received enough from his disability benefits to buy food and some clothes, but not much else. I don't think he's had electricity for quite a while."

"So what's your professional recommendation then?"

"Well, I wouldn't grant him access to the deepest secrets or security features, but I don't see the harm in allowing him to stay. Keep an eye on him, of course, but my initial feeling is that he's unconnected to the rogue dragon-shifters. I think he just wanted to be out of sight, and that was one of the best places to hide."

He nodded. "Keep looking and let me know if you find out anything else. Brenna can't stay on Lochguard forever, so rotate who can be his guard, when needed."

Grant jostled wee Jamie, and he gurgled to himself. The lad was probably the most behaved of anyone in Finn's extended family so far.

Grant spoke again. "There's one more thing, Finn. Things have been hectic, but Bram has requested a video conference with you yet again."

"About the foster candidate?"

"Aye. I'll hold him off as long as I can, but you can't do it forever."

He ran a hand through his hair. He had already agreed to allow a human from the DDA to observe his clan, and he or she should be arriving before too much longer. Now, he needed to settle the business with Stonefire as well. Bram had delayed the process long enough. Finn couldn't do the same after so much badgering.

He also needed to find time to spend with his mate and children, too. "And here I thought my job would get easier with time," he muttered.

Grant shrugged. "It still may. With all your family settled down, they should cause less stress."

Placing a hand on Grant's shoulder, he squeezed. "It's nice to have another levelheaded male in the family." Moving his hand, he chucked wee Jamie's chin. "And I suspect you may be one, too, if your father has anything to say about it. Fergus is usually the most logical one." He met Grant's gaze again. "Speaking of which, the frenzy is still on, aye?"

Grant smiled. "Judging by some of the noise complaints, aye, it is and going well."

"Good. Now, let's head back in. It's time for wee Jamie to meet his newest cousins."

Finn turned around, but Dr. Sid's voice filled his ear. "Finn, a word."

He motioned for Grant to go on ahead into Fraser and Holly's room. Once he was alone with the doctor, he quirked his brows in question.

Sid didn't hesitate. "I have the test results back. Freya is indeed allergic to a number of ingredients, but none of them were in the formula she ate."

His heart stopped beating a second. "Then what's going on?"

"I'm not entirely certain, but Gregor just got off the phone with a colleague in one of the Australian clans—Mirrorbluff. Apparently, two of their bairns have also had flashing dragon eyes. And before you ask, no, they're not sure about why it's happening, either. But at least this tells us that it's not just Freya."

"Gregor is reaching out to other clans as well?" Finn asked.

"As we speak. As soon as I find out more, I'll let you know. For now, just try to keep Freya calm and immediately report any changes in her behavior. I can't really try anything else until I have more information."

As Sid turned back the way she came, Finn took a second in the empty hallway to rub his face. He said to his dragon, *The doctors on Stonefire have just started producing successful antidotes to the drug that turned dragon-shifters rogue or even took their memory. And just when we're ahead, something else pops up.*

It could be connected. But until the doctors find out more, we need to focus on the clan and family. There are many ways to protect them, and we can't neglect any of them.

Aye, aye, I know, dragon. Let's enjoy Fraser and Holly's twins for a bit longer before we tell Ara what Sid disclosed.

Just don't wait too long. Ara deserves to know. With the new knowledge, she may even have a suggestion of why it's happening.

After taking a deep breath, Finn smiled and went back into his cousins' room. The new parents didn't deserve any extra stress, so he'd have to find a way to draw Arabella into a private room without raising suspicion.

His dragon snorted. *Good luck. Aunt Lorna sees everything.*

Ignoring his beast, he went to Arabella's side and tried to think of how to do it.

Chapter Nine

As soon as Finn returned to her side, Arabella sensed the tension in his body. Something had happened.

So after oohing and aahing for about five minutes, she managed to beg Melanie and Tristan to watch the triplets for a short while and all but forced Finn into a private room. The second the door clicked closed, she stated, "Tell me what's going on."

"No keeping anything from you, is there? You would've made a good interrogator."

"Finn," she growled.

With a sigh, he dropped the facade. "When I was talking with Grant in the hall, Dr. Sid showed up."

"And? What did she say?"

"Freya does have a few allergies, but none of them were in the formula. However, two bairns in Australia have shown similar symptoms as hers, with their dragons showing up extremely early and even taking control for a bit."

"Is there anything either the bairns or parents have in common?"

"I don't know. You'd have to ask Sid and Gregor that."

She raised her chin and took his hand. "Then let's find Sid and ask her while we have the chance."

They made their way to where the collection of doctors' offices were kept. Arabella's mind whirled with possibilities and even a bit of hope, but she tried her best to contain it. She needed the facts first, and then she could sort out her feelings.

Arabella finally spotted Sid through the window of one of the doors and knocked.

The doctor let them in. "Finn told you what I found?"

"Yes. And I had a few questions, if you have a moment." Sid stood back and motioned them inside. Gregor was in a corner, talking on a phone, so Arabella kept her voice low. "Has Gregor been able to find out the finer details of each child and parent? We may all have something in common."

She loved that Sid didn't dismiss her statement as foolish. "He's in the middle of assessing that right now. So far, he's only collected information on one of the mothers. Everything is fairly routine, except for a minor incident she had as a teenager." Arabella raised her brows in question and Sid continued, "She became lost and broke her leg. Some humans found her unconscious and took her to a local hospital. They assumed she was human since she was too young for her tattoo, and they treated her as such. The female had a severe reaction to the anesthetic and sedatives they gave her. However, thanks to a nurse who had a cousin mated to a dragon-shifter, he grew suspicious, tested her, and found out that she wasn't human. Because of that nurse, the female managed to survive."

Arabella froze. She and the teenager had something in common. It could be nothing, but it could also be everything.

Her dragon spoke up. *Then just tell her. Sid is always open to information.*

Finn squeezed her hand, and Arabella took strength from the act to spit out, "I was also administered sedatives when I was a teenager."

Recognition flared in Sid's eyes. "When you were captured."

"Yes." Finn released her hand and wrapped an arm around her shoulders. Finn's solid presence at her side gave Arabella the courage to talk about the event. "I woke up groggy the first time, confused and scared. Someone noticed and immediately injected something into my arm. I blacked out again. The second time, they kept me awake. And...and that was when everything else happened."

Since Arabella had known Sid her whole life, the doctor knew to get to the point rather than murmur reassurances. "Did you notice any aftereffects?"

She shook her head. "No. But I was in extreme pain, remember, and scared out of my wits. So they could've been there and I didn't notice. Even afterward, everyone concentrated on keeping me alive so it would've been easy to miss something so minor. Or I could be one of the lucky few who isn't sensitive to human sedatives." Leaning her head on Finn's shoulder, she thought of Freya and forced her voice to be strong. "If the mother of the third child also received human sedatives, then it's possible that's the link."

Which meant Arabella was the reason her daughter was having difficulties. For all she knew, the sedatives could've done something to her body that would affect some or even all of her children.

Her dragon huffed. *Don't place blame on us. Even if it is the link, the drugs were forced upon us.*

Finn squeezed her tighter against him and murmured, "I won't allow you to blame yourself, love. So stop it."

Frowning, Sid shook her head. "Of course this isn't your fault, Arabella. If anything, you may have just given us a way to correct or at least help the situation."

Since she knew neither Sid nor Finn would ever allow

her to keep placing blame, she merely sighed. “If I am the link, then run any and all tests you need to on me, too. I’ll do anything to save my daughter.”

Sid bobbed her head. “I know. And this whole situation is another reason Gregor and I need to forge alliances with other dragon-shifter doctors. If we had access to this information or a place to speak freely with one another, this could’ve been discovered long ago and might even have been preventable.”

Finn spoke up. “Aye, but since most clans keep to themselves, everyone thinks it’s an odd occurrence.”

“Yes,” Sid answered. “But knowledge gives us power, as well as provides more opportunities to try and treat Freya and the others. We don’t have anything yet, but I hope Gregor, Trahern, and I can try to find something to ease or fix the issue. Once we have more confirmation, I’ll probably draw some blood and return to Stonefire. All of our equipment is there, as well as Trahern and Dr. Davies.”

Dr. Emily Davies was a Welsh human, who Arabella had only met a few times. She was temporarily working on Stonefire.

Finn grunted agreement. “And I’m sure Bram will allow you to return here if need be. Do whatever you need to do to help our Freya.”

“As if I would do anything less.” Sid motioned toward a chair. “I may as well draw some blood now, Ara. That way I won’t have to take you away from your children again, at least for the time being.”

Sitting in the chair, Arabella rolled up her sleeve and allowed Sid to do her work. While ensuring Freya had a safe and stable future was her top concern, she couldn’t help but worry if her two sons might also be affected.

Only time would tell.

And she hated the uncertainty.

On the way back to where Melanie and Tristan were watching the triplets, Finn quickly pulled Arabella into a side room. After locking the door, he took her face in his hands. "How are you doing, love?"

For a few seconds, Arabella remained silent. Finn knew his mate occasionally still had bad dreams about her torture as a teenager. No doubt bringing up the memories had shaken her.

Arabella was strong, but sometimes determination wasn't enough to chase away nightmares.

Searching his eyes, she murmured, "Conflicted. I know I can't change what happened to me, and it was done against my will, but I still feel responsible, Finn. I hate to think we brought Freya into the world and doomed her to an unstable future."

He leaned closer. "It's most definitely not your fault, love. Besides, Dr. Sid and the others will sort this out. And then Freya will plot and get into trouble with her cousins, just as any normal child does. I will do whatever it takes to ensure that happens, even if it means searching the Amazon Rainforest for a rare flower or giant insect."

"You hate insects, so that is a fairly big offer."

He growled. "Arabella."

She smiled. "And this, right here, is why I'm not running to a room and hiding from the world like I would've done before. What happened to me as a teen is dark, but you emit more than enough light to chase most of it away."

He kissed her gently. "Then I'll just have to work harder at being even brighter so that there's no darkness whatsoever."

She groaned. "Please tell me that doesn't include you upping your charm. I'm not sure I can take it."

Releasing her face, he pulled her close and nuzzled her cheek with his own. "I have decades of charm left to give you, Ara. And you wouldn't have it any other way."

Before his mate could argue, he kissed her. After slowly nipping her bottom lip and caressing the inside of her mouth, he finally pulled away. "But just remember that charm isn't the only thing in my arsenal. Once Freya and her brothers are safe and free of danger, I'm going to make you forget about your past and all your worries. In our bed."

Arabella's breath hitched, and he knew she'd missed him naked and inside her. Sometimes he wondered why fate required pregnancy with true mates. Finn would've loved a year or two to ensure Arabella knew how much he treasured her.

His dragon huffed. *She is ours. That is all that matters. We have a lifetime together.*

Arabella's voice prevented him from replying to his beast. "I hope you can live up to your promises, Finn. After all, I know how sluggish you can be from lack of sleep. Maybe your gray hairs are telling me something."

He gently slapped her arse cheek. "You've just set down a challenge for me, love."

"Good." She kissed him and continued. "So let's go and find a way to help our children. The sooner we do, the sooner I can see how you try to beat that challenge."

He nearly asked again if she were all right, but restrained himself.

His dragon spoke up. *Good. She is strong. If she needs help, she'll ask us.*

Wrapping an arm around Arabella's waist, he guided them out of the room and to where their triplets were. All he could do was tackle each new obstacle as it appeared.

Chapter Ten

A few days later, Arabella lay awake on the bed next to Finn, keeping an ear out for her children. She'd just finished feeding and changing them. Normally, she'd go back to sleep, but every once in a while, Freya would roar and Arabella would rush to her daughter's side to calm her.

Her dragon yawned. *She's fine for now. Besides, she roars loud enough to wake the dead. You won't sleep through it. There's another reason you're lying awake.*

Her beast was correct, not that she wanted to admit it. *I want to trust Dad, I do. But I still don't know him well enough, especially since he's spent most of his time with us sleeping.*

Mel and Tristan are staying in the second nursery. Our brother won't allow anything bad to happen. Not that I think it will. Our father is just exhausted. Let him sleep.

Finn rolled over and tossed his arm across her chest. His groggy voice filled the room. "Why are you still awake? We have an hour before we have to get up. You should be sleeping."

Cuddling into Finn's side, she traced the shape of the tattoo on his bicep. "Until we can tame Freya's dragon, I'll always be worrying. Shouldn't Sid and Gregor have more information by now?"

"Until the Australian clan run their tests, there's nothing to compare it to. They're doing all they can, love. And you know that."

She remained silent a few beats, never ceasing her finger's movement on his arm. "At least the problem of your family is sorted, so that's something. Holly and Fraser have settled in, and Gina and Fergus are still in the frenzy. Even Faye has been behaving herself, probably because she's so tired as a result of taking care of Mac-squared."

"Aye, they're in line for the moment. We'll see if it lasts." He kissed her cheek, his faint stubble tickling her skin. "However, I would handle them a million times over if it meant Freya's dragon was forever stable and under control."

Her daughter's dragon had appeared more times than Arabella would've liked.

Turning her face to kiss Finn and reassure him as much as herself, a thunderous roar stopped her from doing so. "Freya."

They both jumped out of bed, and Arabella rushed to the room next to theirs. Switching on the light, her heart skipped a beat.

Instead of a human baby laying in Freya's crib, there was a baby gold dragon.

Her first thought was to sob—few children who shifted so young ever shifted back.

But her dragon growled. *She is* our *daughter. She can overcome anything.*

Finn murmured in a soothing voice, "That's my lass, a gold dragon like your dad."

Freya moved her head to meet her father's gaze, letting out a small roar.

Since Finn was better at calming their daughter than her, Arabella stayed where she was and watched both of them closely.

Finn took another step and put out a hand. "That was an impressive roar as well, for one so young. I'm sure you'll have all the lads fuming they can't do a roar like you, Freya."

The baby dragon didn't roar again, so Finn took another step. It took everything Arabella had not to rush over and scoop up her daughter.

Putting his hand in front of Freya's snout, Finn murmured, "Let me pet my fiery lass, aye?"

Arabella dug her nails into her palm so hard they probably drew blood. But she stood still, waiting to see what Freya would do.

After a few more beats, she bumped her snout against Finn's hand. He moved to scratch behind her tiny ears. "Aye, there's nothing like a good ear scratch, especially when you're wee. I remember how flaky my skin was as a lad."

Freya met her dad's eyes before hunching down and jumping into Finn's arms.

As their daughter cuddled against Finn's chest, he murmured, "Call Layla."

She was torn between staying and doing as he asked.

Her beast spoke up. *Finn will take care of her. We need Layla's help.*

Before she could change her mind, Arabella raced into the hall and into her and Finn's room. She picked up her mobile and dialed Layla.

The doctor picked up on the second ring. "Arabella? What's wrong?"

"Freya's shifted into her dragon form."

Thankfully Layla's voice remained strong, which helped keep Arabella from panicking. "I'll be there straight away. I'll call Sid on the way, too, just in case she's learned anything since last evening."

"Hurry, Layla."

"I will, Ara. Staying strong and collected is the best thing you can do for the bairn."

The line went dead and Arabella lowered her phone. Melanie's soft voice came from the doorway. "Is everything okay, Ara? We heard the running."

Arabella explained the situation and added, "I know it's a lot to ask, but can you keep the twins occupied? I don't want their own inner dragons to come out and think to try the same thing."

Melanie engulfed her in a hug. "Of course. They're still asleep in the second nursery, with Tristan watching over them. I just wish there was something else we could do."

Leaning back, she met her sister-in-law's eyes. "As much as you hate it, you can't fix everything, Mel."

"Just make sure you realize that, too, Ara. Have faith in the doctors and everything will work out. No one is better at finding a solution and cure than Dr. Sid."

Swallowing back the emotion choking her throat, she bobbed her head. "I know."

Melanie smoothed back Arabella's hair. "Then go to your daughter. Tristan and I will protect the rest of your family for as long as you need."

After one more quick hug, Arabella raced back to where Finn and Freya should be. However, as soon as she entered the room, she stopped and tried not to panic.

Finn and Freya were nowhere to be found.

In most any other situation, Finn would be laughing at himself being stuck in a hedge just below the nursery window.

However, the present was no laughing matter.

Freya had jumped from his arms to the window, glanced at him, and launched into the air.

At that moment, his heart had leapt from his chest.

But then he'd seen her flap her small wings a few times before crashing into a hedge. The second he'd seen her emerge and acting as if everything were normal, there'd been no other alternative but for Finn to do the same and jump out the window.

As he struggled to free himself from the blasted thing, Freya was already on the ground going in circles, chasing her tail.

Finally dislodging himself from the hedge, he walked slowly to Freya, debating what to do. Because if her dragon were in charge, she might think it was a game and he could be chasing her forever.

His beast spoke up. *I still say we should shift. Even a wee dragon without any sense will listen to a much bigger one. And I am one of the biggest ones on Lochguard.*

He ignored his dragon's ego to focus on what was more important. *It could also scare her. Ara and I haven't had time to shift into our dragon forms and introduce you to the bairns yet.*

And who's fault is that?

Finn mentally sighed. *I promise to listen to you more once this is sorted. For now, work with me, aye?*

His dragon grunted. *Then shift.*

Arabella's voice drifted from the window above. "Finn? What's going on?"

Freya looked up at her mother before dashing toward the back of the garden.

Finn answered, "Trust me," before shucking his clothes and imagining his nose elongating into a snout, his fingers turning into talons, and wings growing from his back. Within seconds, he stood in his golden dragon form.

His dragon spoke up. *Let me take charge and try first.*

Moving to the back of their mind, Finn did as asked.

His beast walked slowly toward Freya, who was now trying to catch a bug in her jaw. If there weren't any danger to his only daughter, Finn would think the scene adorable.

His dragon grunted and Freya paused with her mouth open. After another grunt, the little dragon met his eyes.

He roared gently and motioned toward the house.

Freya dashed into the waist-high grass at the very back of the garden.

His dragon spoke inside their mind. *I think she wants to play. Let's try it.*

Trusting his beast, Finn said nothing.

Freya popped her head up and then ducked down with a squeal. She may not be able to do the same in her human form for quite a while, but baby dragons could walk from birth. It was yet another reason why it was best that they usually didn't shift until they were older. Otherwise, parents would go mad a lot sooner.

His dragon silently stood still. Finn wanted to shout for his dragon to get on with it, but resisted. His other half had never let him down before.

After what seemed like hours, his dragon darted down their head and gently took hold of the back of Freya's neck. As he lifted the wee one, she remained frozen. Finn asked, *How did you know to do that?*

Instinct. Dragons aren't the only ones to use this method to fetch their young.

Cats did it, too, for one. But Finn wasn't about to compare his dragon to a wee, scruffy beastie.

His dragon carefully swung them around and plodded toward the cottage. Because of their height, they easily deposited Freya into Arabella's outstretched arms, who still stood at the nursery window.

His mate instantly cuddled Freya close and murmured, "Don't do that again, love. Jumping out of windows isn't okay."

Freya grunted, and Finn would've laughed if he'd been in human form. He had a feeling Arabella would want bars on the windows within the week.

Not that he had time to dwell on that for long. Layla raced into the garden and poked Finn's side. "Take me up there."

His beast spoke up. *I'm not a ladder or crane.*

Just do it, dragon. For Freya's sake.

Fine, although I think Freya just wanted to play.

His dragon scooped up Layla with one forelimb and carefully deposited her on the window sill.

As soon as the doctor was inside, Finn imagined his wings shrinking, his snout returning to his nose and face, and his tail disappearing into his body. The second he was human again, he snatched his clothes, headed for the door, and raced up the stairs.

Arabella held Freya's little dragon form against her body and willed her heart to slow down.

She had her baby girl again, but the situation was far from stable.

Although as Layla crawled into the room, Arabella had to sit in the chair. Her little girl wasn't so little in her dragon form and probably weighed at least fifty pounds.

Layla crouched down to be eye level with Freya and said with a smile, "You may be the only female, but you've taken after your dad, haven't you? I can imagine him doing the same as a lad. We're almost the same age, after all. So I have lots of stories to tell you when you're older."

Arabella knew Layla was trying to charm Freya, but she

could help but blurt, "Have you found out anything new?"

Layla switched her gaze to Arabella and continued to smile. "Maybe. Sid and Gregor think that the sedatives affected certain hormones in your body, which then created imbalances in your bairns. If they're right, then dispensing medication once a month or so until they're mature should keep the young dragons in their hiding spots inside the mind. At least, until they're mature enough to come out around the same time as everyone else, when they're five or six years old. We'll have to see how it goes after that, as maybe the imbalances will sort themselves out as they mature."

Arabella moved her gaze to her daughter and scratched behind one of her ears. Freya leaned into the touch and Arabella hesitated. Freya was so happy in her dragon form. What would happen if she took it away? She might resent her forever.

And yet, if she allowed Freya's dragon to come out as she pleased, it could end up turning her daughter rogue.

Her beast spoke up. *Freya is clever. Maybe we can teach her dragon to shift back. If it fails, then use the medication to tame the dragon half.*

It could be disastrous, and yet...

You want to talk with Finn and maybe try it, her dragon finished.

She looked back at Layla. "Once Sid has more information, let us know. I need to talk to Finn first."

Bobbing her head, Layla stood. "Of course, but I'm still going to check on the triplets daily for now. If it becomes dangerous, we might have to subdue their dragons, Ara. I know she seems happy, but if she turns rogue, then you could lose her forever."

Or, worse, the Department of Dragon Affairs could take her away and throw her in jail.

Some might cry or lash out at Layla's honesty, but Arabella took comfort in it. "You're becoming a fantastic doctor, Layla. I can't wait to see what you accomplish in the future."

Layla's pale cheeks flushed pink. "I'm just doing my job."

"You are, but remember to take time for you as well. Working yourself to death won't help anyone."

Layla somehow worked more than Finn ever had before the triplets had been born, and Arabella worried about her. Especially since she knew that Chase McFarland—the younger brother of Grant—found every opportunity to drop in on Layla at the surgery and invite her out. Arabella thought a bit of fun would do the doctor good. Too bad Layla seemed not to notice the male's attention.

However, before she could suggest anything, Layla moved to the doorway. "Make sure she shifts back before too much longer. Watching her dad do it might help. I just don't want to risk her liking her form too much and then never changing back."

Freya yawned and curled into a ball on Arabella's lap.

Well, she attempted to curl into a ball. Arabella's lap wasn't quite big enough, and it was more like she leaned against her chest and spilled onto her lap.

Finn appeared right behind Layla. "Aye, I'll give it a try once she wakes up. She deserves a wee nap after her recent adventure."

With a nod, Layla left them alone.

Her mate came to stand at her side and gently scratched Freya's ears. "She hasn't been acting rogue yet, Ara. Everything might work out."

Glancing up at her mate, she asked, "How much did you hear?"

"All of it." Putting an arm around Arabella's shoulder, she leaned against him. He continued, "And I agree that we should give Freya a chance. She's intelligent for her age and just wants to play. Considering she can't even roll over yet in her human form, I can't blame her."

They both watched their little girl sleep, her chest rising and falling with each breath. She was safe for the moment, and that was all that mattered.

Deciding to lighten the mood and lower her blood pressure, Arabella murmured, "Figures she'd be a gold dragon and not purple."

"Aye, well, gold dragons have a sparkle about them after all. The lads might take after their old dad as well."

"I'd like to think that they'll be purple like me," Arabella replied. "I know it's rare for male dragons to be purple, but that would make them that much more special."

Finn chuckled. "Our sons, the next generation of dragon models."

She snorted. "Let's hope not. Male egos are big enough. If everyone fawns over them from a young age? They'll become unbearable."

Finn hugged her against him. "Between you, Faye, and Aunt Lorna, I don't think we'll have to worry about that. Besides, Holly and Fraser's twin females could do with a set of rivals. I'm starting to warm up to the idea of Dec and Gray being purple."

"The clan will most likely think you and your cousins are trying to take over the world, especially with two sets of rarities in one generation. I'm sure tales will be sung about it one day."

"Aye, I rather like the sound of that." She rolled her eyes and Finn laughed. "It's all hypothetical, love. Our sons could be polka dot for all I care, as long as we're together."

Maybe when her children were older, she could play a prank on Finn. Putting washable paint on their dragon hides and watching Finn wonder if they had some new disease might be fun.

Her dragon chuckled. *You're becoming a bit devious.*

I like to think of it as keeping Finn on his toes.

Her beast laughed as she curled up at the back of her mind.

Arabella enjoyed a moment of peace, leaning against her mate and cuddling her daughter. They might have some tough decisions to make soon enough, but they could wait a little while longer.

CHAPTER ELEVEN

George MacLeod sat on his bed and resisted rubbing the stubs of his legs.

With all the running and shouting, he knew something wasn't right. Part of him wanted to go check on Arabella to make sure everything was okay.

But then he remembered how he'd abandoned her and Tristan, so he stayed put. His daughter now had a mate to protect her. George's window for redemption was gone.

After years of suppressing his inner dragon, the beast rarely spoke up. However, he sat at the back of George's mind and grunted.

Not dignifying his dragon with a response, George ran a hand down his face and glanced at his prosthetics and debated putting them on. With all the commotion, it would be easy enough to slip away. That would give Arabella one less thing to worry about.

A knock on the door made him jump. Tristan's voice came through the door. "I hear you in there. I'm coming in."

His son entered and shut the door behind him. Crossing his arms, Tristan studied him.

George looked away.

He'd failed his son just as much as his daughter.

Tristan growled. "If you're going to leave again, then just

do it. The longer you stay, the more Arabella will get her hopes up. And while Finn is her mate and can protect her with most things, I will protect her from you, if need be."

Silence fell. George had no defense.

Maybe it would be better if he left.

His dragon did speak up. *Our grandchildren.*

Before he could decide whether to reply to his beast or not, another knock sounded. From the corner of his eye, George saw a human male in his sixties enter. George had seen him once before, but didn't recall his name.

The male spoke with a Scottish accent. "Tristan, leave us be."

"You're human, Ross. It's not a smart idea to be left alone with George. In a physical fight, he'd still win."

"I know what I'm doing, lad. Leave us."

Tristan didn't move. After a few beats, he sighed. "It seems like our clans are full of stubborn humans these days. But I'll be right outside the door. That's not up for negotiation."

Tristan left and the human male spoke again. "I'm not scary, George. At least look at me, aye? I'm a wee bit more interesting than the floor."

Out of curiosity, he glanced at the smiling male. The human was entirely too cheerful for George's liking.

Not that he had a chance to say anything, even if he wanted. Ross sat next to him on the bed and continued. "You don't know me, but we have something in common, you and me. My wife was murdered as well."

That piqued George's curiosity. "But I saw you with her a few days ago."

"No, that's my second wife, Lorna. I lost my first wife, Anne, many years ago. She was murdered by a stalker."

"That's not the same at all," he bit out.

Ross raised his brows. "How so? She reported the stalker, but the police did nothing. I could've moved away, and I didn't. For the longest time, I blamed myself." Ross fell quiet for a few beats before adding, "It took loving Lorna to realize there was little I could've done. From everything I've heard about your wife, there's little you could've done yourself. She was flying with Arabella to a hunting site, aye? And the hunters attacked them en route."

At Ross's words, George closed his eyes. He'd imagined the situation a thousand times, and each time he wanted to rip his heart out of his chest if it meant he could switch places with Jocelyn.

He finally replied, "Even if both of us couldn't have prevented what happened to our females, what I did afterward was worse."

Ross looked away and clasped his hands together. "Staying after my wife's death wasn't easy. But even so, there's something you're overlooking."

The human's confidence sparked irritation inside of him. "And that is?"

Meeting his eyes, Ross stated, "You stayed until Arabella pulled through. I'm not a doctor, but I bet that saved her life. So, aye, running away was shameful. But at least you helped your daughter when she needed it most. She is here today partly because of you, and not just because you shagged her mother, either."

The human was strange, and George ignored his reference to Arabella's conception. "It's not that simple. My son told me how Ara suffered for nearly a decade afterward. My running away played a big part of that."

"Perhaps. But you're here now, staying in your daughter's house. Ara used to be a lonely lass, but she has more love and family than ever before. However, I'm of the opinion that she could always use a wee bit more, especially from a father she assumed was dead." Ross stood. "If you ever need to talk and sort out yourself regarding what happened to your mate, come find me. However, only you can find the will to live and start over with your children. The question is whether you want to forever punish yourself and deny your grandchildren a relationship, or are you going to face your fears and guilt to maybe have love in your life again. The choice is up to you."

With that, Ross left the room.

As George sat alone on his bed, a flicker of hope flashed in his chest. Ross could be talking out of his arse, but George's gut said he wasn't.

Although why a human Scot would care about his happiness, George had no idea.

His dragon whispered, *You've forgotten, but I haven't. It was like this many years ago on Stonefire.*

George knew full well he didn't have the strength to face everyone on Stonefire.

At least, not yet.

He blinked. Where had that thought come from?

His dragon said, *I say fight. I will help.*

Considering his beast hadn't offered to help in over a decade, George did pause at that.

He rubbed his face. He had no idea why so many people were trying to help him, an English stranger. But for some reason, their optimism and determination were starting to wear off on him.

For the first time, George considered fighting to be the male his children and grandchildren deserved. The only problem was, he didn't know if he was strong enough to do it or not.

CHAPTER TWELVE

Arabella awoke the next morning, the sun streaming in through the window of the nursery.

Finn must've allowed her to sleep and had used her frozen breast milk to feed the twins.

Speaking of which, if she didn't find a baby soon, her breasts would burst.

The heavy weight of Freya's dragon wasn't on her chest, but when Arabella glanced down, she froze.

Freya slept in Arabella's arms, but she was in her human form.

Relief crashed over her and she blinked back tears. At least for now, her daughter was safe.

Swallowing back her emotions so as to not wake her daughter, she finally noticed that someone had tossed a blanket over Freya. Ever so slowly, Arabella lifted it and saw that her daughter was naked but for a nappy.

Her beast spoke up. *Maybe Finn got her to shift and brought her back.*

And I slept through it all. I'm not a very good mother.

Stop it. Of course we are. If Finn is near, we know things are all right.

She took a moment to gently trace her daughter's cheek. If Freya had indeed shifted back easily, then maybe they'd never have to use the medication on her and banish her dragon.

After watching her sleeping daughter for who knew how long, Arabella finally decided it was time to get up and find the rest of her family.

She managed to stand and exit the nursery without waking Freya. As she made her way toward the stairs, the smell of pancakes and bacon filled her nose.

Her stomach rumbled, and Arabella moved as quickly as she could without jostling her baby. She hadn't eaten much since Freya had woken up with slitted dragon eyes. She might just have to kiss whoever was making breakfast.

However, as soon as she entered the kitchen and dining area, she stilled in her tracks.

Her father was at the cooker, flipping a pancake. Tristan and Melanie each had one of Arabella's sons, offering them various toys to keep them entertained.

Finn was at George's side, issuing instructions on when to flip the pancakes.

Considering the last time she'd seen her father, he'd barely muttered a few sentences and had kept his gaze trained on the ground, she wondered what had caused the transformation.

Finn noticed her first. "Good morning, love. I hope you're hungry. We have enough food to feed an army."

At her mate's cheerful tone, she smiled. "You mean barely enough to feed the MacKenzies, then."

"Ah, but I didn't invite them over, so we have enough for ourselves for a change." Finn patted her father's shoulder. "Your dad here has been a huge help. He actually came down first and was trying to find everything. So I decided to help. Your brother and Mel came at the first scent of bacon."

Tristan grunted. "More like your sons were crying and

hungry. Unlike you lot, I don't eat to excess."

Melanie rolled her eyes. "You smelled the bacon first, and your getting up woke the twins."

"Mel," Tristan growled.

"Hey, it's true." She grinned at Arabella. "Speaking of your sons, I'm not sure how you manage to feed all three of your babies. These two could probably eat an entire cow and still be hungry."

"Good, because I need to feed one of them and I don't want to wake Freya. Speaking of which, when did she change back?"

Finn came over and took their daughter. Freya snuggled into Finn's chest and went slack again. "She did it on her own," he murmured.

Melanie handed over Declan and Arabella took him. "What?"

Motioning with his head, Finn said softly, "Sit, Ara, and I'll tell you everything. Because if you don't start feeding that lad, Dec is going to scream bloody murder with the food source so close."

In any other situation, Arabella would've rolled her eyes and made a quip. But she settled down and got Declan nursing before looking back at her mate. "Well? What happened?"

Finn kissed Freya's forehead before answering, "Aunt Lorna and Ross came over last night, after someone told her of the commotion. In the time I went to answer the door and bring my aunt to the nursery, Freya had shifted back. Since I didn't want her to piss all over you, I risked putting a nappy on. And the little one slept through it the entire time. I suppose jumping out of a window is exhausting to a bairn."

Declan wrapped his tiny fingers around Arabella's forefinger as he continued to nurse. "More like she's taken after you and is out to prove to the world how clever she is."

Her father's voice filled the room. "Or, she has your stubbornness."

Her gaze shot to her father's, and while her dad wasn't smiling, she didn't see the pity and self-hatred from before.

Something must've happened, but Arabella wasn't going to question it right now. "Which would be your fault, as Tristan and I inherited that from you."

She resisted holding her breath as she waited for her dad to respond. She hated walking on eggshells around him. But she more than any knew that change didn't come instantly.

Her dad answered, "That's what your mother always said, too."

Tears threatened to fall at the mention of her mother, but she held them back. Crying might send her father scurrying back into his room again. "Well, I think Freya has it as well. We have yet to see about the boys, although I suspect they may be even worse." She paused and finally blurted out, "Dec is finished. Did you want to sit and burp him, Dad?"

Finn moved Freya to his shoulder and kept their daughter there with one arm. "I can take over pancake duties. I've become quite skilled at doing things one-handed."

If Fraser had been in the room, Arabella knew the conversation would've turned to the gutter. And part of her wished all her family could be here, too. More than anyone, the MacKenzies could lighten the mood and make someone feel at ease.

Well, after a person recovered from the initial shock at the MacKenzies' behavior. But in the end, everyone at least smiled with them in the room, bickering and fighting as usual.

And her dad could sorely use some more smiles and maybe even laughter.

Her dragon spoke up. *Soon. We don't want to over-*

whelm Dad just yet.

Knowing Aunt Lorna, we'll all be over for dinner this evening anyway, even with Fergus and Gina still in the frenzy.

Her father's voice prevented her beast from replying. "I'm glad you're talking with your dragon again."

"Me, too." She motioned to a seat next to her. As soon as her father maneuvered into the chair, she proffered Dec. "This baby loves attention, so you shouldn't have any problems with him."

Declan gave a few "ahh, ahh, ahh" sounds and her dad smiled.

The sight reminded her of when she was a child, and her dad would smile before picking her up and tossing her into the air.

Maybe he'd be that way again in the future.

As her father placed Declan over his shoulder and gently patted his back, Melanie brought over Grayson and said, "I think next time we need to bring the twins. Annabel tends to dominate the other children her age, but I think your kids might give her a run for her money."

Settling Grayson at her other breast, she snorted. "You are aware that they're only a few months old, right?"

Melanie motioned toward Freya. "But if she changes into a dragon, I bet it'll awe my daughter. At least, for a minute or two. And maybe that will convince her that she's not the strongest little dragon-shifter to ever walk the earth."

Tristan grunted. "More likely it'll give her ideas."

Melanie waved a hand in dismissal. "I doubt she'll be able to defy instinct and bring out her dragon."

"She's half-human, so anything is possible. After all, you defied the odds. I'm sure our children will do the same."

"And is that a bad thing?"

Tristan sighed. "It just means trouble is coming."

As Melanie and Tristan continued to argue, Arabella smiled and glanced over at her father. He hummed a tune as he burped Declan and met her gaze. He gave a slight nod and Arabella returned the gesture.

All signs pointed to her dad deciding to fight. And if Finn could find a way for him to stay long-term, her family might grow yet again.

And to Arabella, who had once had almost no family and thought she'd die alone, it raised her spirits. She would never be able to see her mother again or meet Finn's parents, but she would never be without someone loving her.

Chapter Thirteen

Fergus MacKenzie stared at Gina's sleeping face and couldn't stop smiling.

His mate carried his child.

He had no idea how many days had passed during the frenzy, but more than enough had gone by to wear out his wee human. Ever since his dragon had told him she carried his scent, meaning she was pregnant, Fergus had wanted to pull her close and hold her.

But she deserved some sleep after how many times he and his dragon had taken her, so he let her rest.

His beast yawned. *You don't have to worry about the frenzy any longer. If you pull her close, she'll probably just fall right back asleep.*

I don't want to chance it.

Gina's sleepy voice filled the room. "I can feel you staring at me, Fergus." She opened her eyes. "Is something wrong?"

Running a finger down her cheek, he answered, "Nothing is wrong, lass. The frenzy is finished and you need the rest."

Gina sat up confidently, not bashful about her nakedness. Fergus should be the gentleman, but he couldn't help but glance down at her glorious breasts.

"Fergus." He met her gaze and she frowned. "What do

you mean the frenzy is finished?"

Raising a hand, he lightly played with her nipple. "You carry my scent, which means you carry my child."

She batted his hand away and moved hers to cover her belly. "I'm pregnant?"

"Aye." He covered her hand with his. "I'm sorry it's so soon after wee Jamie, lass. But I'm also happy I don't have to worry about doing this anymore."

He pulled her close and hugged her against him.

Many people took the simple act of holding a loved one for granted. However, Fergus had denied both of them the luxury for weeks, so he closed his eyes and savored his female's heat against him.

Kissing the top of Gina's head, he finally murmured, "I love you, Gina."

She snuggled into his chest. "Oh, Fergus. I love you, too. And I hope you know that I'm going to be glued to your side for a little while. I've missed my dragonman."

"You were only asleep for half an hour, love."

She lightly hit his chest. "You know what I mean. Maybe I should start using Jane Hartley's phrase of dragon cuddles." Leaning her head back, she met his eyes. "Promise me that you'll listen to me more from now on. I enjoy protection as much as the next person, but if you try to shut me out again, I'll leave. I need you to be open and honest with me, but also value my input, too."

His dragon grunted. *Don't you dare lose her.*

Ignoring his beast, he cupped her face with his hands and searched her gaze. "I just hated the thought of losing you, lass. I know the doctors said you endured childbirth easier than any human they'd seen with a dragon-shifter mate before, but that doesn't mean you're invincible."

"Oh, Fergus. I'm not about to go anywhere. After all, if I leave you alone to raise our children, they'll never be allowed to run and play like normal kids."

"Of course they would be allowed to, provided they have several supervisors to watch over them."

She laughed. "See? That's why I have to survive childbirth. I need to conspire with your siblings on how to insert a little fun." Putting up a hand, she added, "Fun with some limitations. I'm not like your brother Fraser."

"I'm sure Fraser will change somewhat once he's a father." He kissed Gina gently. When he finally pulled away, he murmured, "As much as I miss wee Jamie, I wish I could have another week alone with you so that we can enjoy each other. I've missed my lass as well. Not just the physical, either, but simply talking with you, too."

Closing the distance between their lips, Gina took his in a slow, lingering kiss. When she broke it, her hot breath danced against his lips. "We'll figure out some way to have a little alone time before our second child is born. But for now, we should probably see how everyone else is doing. After all, Holly might've given birth by now."

"And no one barged in to tell us?"

She raised her red eyebrows. "And if they had tried?"

He sighed, because Gina was right; he would've kicked them out instantly. "Fair point." After one more kiss, he looped an arm around one of Gina's shoulders and opened the small drawer on the nightstand next to their bed. After plucking out his mobile phone, he glanced at his mate. "I just want to check and make sure everything is all right. Is that okay, lass?"

Gina rolled her eyes. "I'm not a delicate flower that requires every second of your attention. I'll continue to snuggle my dragonman as you make sure both of our families are fine. I trust that our son is behaving more than my sister right now. If she's not careful, she's going to cause a fight between some of the younger dragonmen."

Fergus switched on his phone and grunted. "I've tried telling your sister that flirting with every dragonman who looks her way isn't wise. But she's either going deaf or enjoys the attention."

Gina sighed. "She has always enjoyed getting attention from men. I was hoping Finn would assign her a personal tutor on the ways of dragon-shifters, and that might help her understand the trouble she could cause. Unfortunately, Finn has had a lot going on."

"I'll make sure it happens sooner rather than later." His phone turned on and he clicked his text messages. There were messages from every member of his family, and then some.

After reading the first one, he froze. Gina peered at his face. "What's wrong?"

"Fraser and Holly had twin females."

Patting his chest, she murmured, "Good. Freya could use some female cousins. But I sense there's something you're not telling me."

Fergus explained the stories of twin females being good luck and bringing on change before adding, "I'm not sure if Fraser is going to play it up and soak up the attention, or if he's going to keep his children locked up and out of danger."

"Don't worry, I'm sure all of us can help with that. Faye will especially be determined to make sure his babies get into trouble and I can help her."

Fergus raised an eyebrow. "I'm not sure you want to step into that lifelong war of pranks and tricks."

"Oh, come on. There's nothing wrong with a little fun. You were that way as a child, or so your mother says." Laying her head on Fergus's shoulder, they sat in silence for a few minutes before she spoke again. "I can tell you miss them, Fergus. How about we shower and visit? And not just because I miss our son. I miss everyone."

"They're going to fuss over you, lass. Be prepared."

"More than you already do?"

"Maybe not quite that much, but a fair bit."

She grinned at him. "I could always play it up and see how far they'll take it."

At the way her eyes crinkled when she smiled, his heart skipped a beat, and he forgot all about their conversation. "You're so beautiful."

She searched his gaze. "You already had me many times over. There's no need for compliments to get into my pants."

He threaded the fingers of one hand through her hair. "I mean it, Gina. You're beautiful."

"And you're quite the catch yourself." She gently stroked his bare chest. "How about we take a long shower and then head out?"

"You must be sore, lass. I'll help you wash and promise to leave you alone."

"I want you, Fergus. After so many months of strain, I want the chance to take it slow. Maybe even make you come once with my mouth."

His dragon growled, *Yes.*

Before he could answer, Gina slid out of bed and glanced over her shoulder. "It's your call, dragonman. But now's the time to prove you're listening to me. Because right now, I want you. End of story."

As Gina sauntered across the room and into the attached bathroom, Fergus didn't hesitate to get out of bed and follow her.

After all, he couldn't disappoint his female. If she said she wanted to suck his cock, he was all too happy to oblige.

Of course, Fergus had a few surprises of his own for her. But he didn't think she'd complain.

Chapter Fourteen

Finn surveyed the fourteen adults and six bairns crammed cheek and jowl around Aunt Lorna's dining table and decided that for future family dinners, he might have to use the Great Hall.

His dragon snorted. *As if Lorna would tolerate using any kitchen but her own.*

As Fraser elbowed him on one side by accident, and Arabella did the same on the other, he mentally sighed. *She might not have a choice. I don't think even a double-decker dining table would be enough.*

Then have Fraser design an extension to the house. I'm sure everyone will chip in to have it built.

Aunt Lorna finally entered, with Ross on her heels, and placed the roast on the table. "It's not an entire cow, so this will have to be enough. Which means, no wasting the meat."

Ross put a giant bowl of potatoes down next to the roast. "More than that, let's not give the bairns any ideas about using their food for anything but eating. Maybe the next generation will have some table manners."

Tristan muttered, "Maybe we shouldn't bring our children up here next time."

Arabella spoke up. "Do you want them flying off on their own or maybe tossing a few rolls? I think tossing food is the lesser evil of the two."

Fraser tossed a roll into the air and caught it. "Besides, there's a strategy to it. Even Faye knows that."

Faye snuggled into Grant's side. "Aye, you only toss what you're willing to lose. I'm surprised Mum hasn't learned that over the years. Because making less food would mean fewer fights."

Lorna put a hand on her hip. "I deduced that when you were barely out of nappies, Faye Cleopatra. But as Ara said, I'd much rather deal with a wee bit of trouble in my house than foolish expeditions across the English Channel, or some such nonsense."

Fergus chuckled, his arm around Gina at his side, his fingers lightly tracing shapes on her bicep. "We have a few of those adventures you don't know about, Mum. Maybe someday, we'll share them."

Gina bounced wee Jamie on her lap. "Besides, we may not have to worry about any extra food once all the boys are grown up. Declan and Grayson already eat twice as much as wee Jamie here. If Faye and Grant have twin boys, too, then they'll definitely be less food around to waste."

Faye raised her eyebrows. "Don't dismiss the lasses. I usually eat more than Fergus or Fraser. At the rate this family keeps growing, we're going to leave each meal hungry before too much longer, unless Mum takes up a collection for the grocery bills."

Lorna opened her mouth, but Chase McFarland—Grant's younger brother—grinned and beat her to it. "Then maybe we should plan in advance and bring extra things to use as ammunition. That way we can eat and have a little fun without wasting any of Aunt Lorna's delicious cooking."

Chase flashed a smile at Lorna and Finn glanced at Grant. They shared a look—Chase was nearly as bad a flirt as Gina's sister, Kaylee. Good thing they kept them on opposite sides of the table or Finn might start rolling his eyes nonstop at their continuous banter.

Grant and Chase's mother, Gillian, sighed. "Chase, we're guests in Lorna's house. Don't suggest bringing food to toss about."

Chase shrugged. "Oh, come on, Mum. You laugh along with everyone else, so there's no need for the pretenses of formality and manners."

Gillian opened her mouth, but one of Fraser's daughters started crying. Holly murmured to her mate, "Take Summer into the hall to calm her."

With a sigh, Fraser inched his chair back and managed to squeeze himself out of the chair, all with a tiny newborn in his arms. Once he was outside the room, Holly smiled. "I think our daughters are on my side. It should help with the madness, Lorna."

"Aye, well, we'll see about that." She looked at Ross. "Will you carve? I'm knackered and just want to eat and cuddle one of my grandbabies."

Ross picked up the knife and prongs, but turned them around and held them out to George MacLeod. "I think George should do it. I'm worn out from carrying twenty pounds of potatoes around all day."

All eyes turned toward George. For a second, the male didn't move or say anything. Then he tried to lift himself up, but with the crowded table, he couldn't manage it.

Finn was about to hand off the son in his lap and help him, but Gillian McFarland, sitting to one side of George, stood first.

She offered her arm. For a few beats, George did nothing. Then he finally took Gillian's help and managed to stand.

George murmured, "Thank you."

"Any time," Gillian said with a smile.

The pair stared at each other for a second, some understanding passing between them that Finn couldn't decode.

Then George leaned against the table for support, released his grip on Gillian's arm, and took the utensils from Ross.

As he carved up the roast, Arabella nudged Finn's side. He met her gaze. At the happiness and hope he saw there, his heart swelled.

Even though Freya's future may still be uncertain, as well as their boys' or even George MacLeod's, in that moment, Arabella was happy.

And to Finn, that was the most precious thing in the world. It also only made him want to work harder to keep her this way. He wasn't sure how he'd do it, but for the chance of her smiles and laughter, he would try his hardest. Arabella was a precious gift, and one he'd never take for granted.

EPILOGUE

A Few Weeks Later

Arabella looked down at her three sleeping children and willed her feet to move. She'd kissed each of them goodbye, as well as checked five times that Lorna and Ross had enough supplies for the night.

Her dragon spoke up. *It's okay. Freya only shifts when you or Finn are near. I don't think she'll change the pattern now.*

And if she does?

They have some of Dr. Sid's experimental medication. And even if that fails, Layla will use a diluted dragon slumber drug. Freya will not *go rogue.*

At her side, Lorna spoke up. "It's all right, child. I know what I'm doing. Besides, you and Finn deserve a wee break. What with your father visiting Melanie, Tristan, and their twins, you have no excuse not to enjoy some time with your mate."

Arabella hesitated and her beast sighed. *She's right. Besides, it's been too long since we had our mate. We're healed and ready. And I want to see what he has planned as a surprise.*

She touched the head of each of her children in turn. "Be

good for Mummy and listen to your grandmother."

Her triplets continued to sleep.

Part of her wanted them to make a fuss at her departure, but another part was glad for Lorna's help.

Lorna touched her arm. "Go and see what Finn has planned for you, lass."

"You know what it is?"

"A bit. However, I'd rather not know the details."

Lorna's words piqued her curiosity. After a few more seconds of staring at her babies, Arabella turned toward the front door. "Call if anything happens. I don't care if Finn brought in the human British Queen to our cottage as part of his surprise, my babies come first."

Smiling, Lorna pushed her toward the door. "Aye, I know. But we'll be fine. Faye and Grant are supposed to come over in the morning to help, too."

Taking a deep breath, Arabella bobbed her head. "Thanks, Aunt Lorna. I'll be here tomorrow afternoon."

"Take your time, child."

With that, Arabella exited Lorna and Ross's cottage and walked briskly toward her own.

With each step, her worry was replaced with another emotion—nervousness. Finn had been patient with her, even though the doctor had cleared Arabella for sex two weeks ago. She craved her male, but carrying and birthing triplets had changed her body. She hoped Finn wouldn't be disappointed.

Her dragon huffed. *Of course not. He loves us as we are.*

Ignoring her dragon, Arabella quickly reached her home. But as soon as she could see the front door, she stopped and blinked.

A giant picture of a kitten with rainbows behind it was taped to the door.

Memories of her early courtship rushed back, and she

smiled. Finn had once threatened to leave a pile of rainbow kittens on her front step.

While it was less than a year ago, it seemed like a lifetime. So much had happened between then and now.

Curiosity took over and she forgot about her nervousness. Arabella reached the door and entered the house.

Instead of more rainbows and kittens, there was a giant, pink stuffed unicorn smiling up at her from the floor.

Another thing Finn had threatened her with. Well, if threaten was even the right word. Although Arabella detested pink, so maybe it was.

Picking up the stuffed beast, she noticed sprigs of heather on the floor, leading up the stairs.

Instinctively, she touched her chest where Finn had pinned some heather during their early days. She hadn't known it at the time, but it had let everyone on Lochguard know she was Finn's true mate.

At the top of the stairs was a picture propped on a stand, of her and Finn on their mating day. Another stand had a picture of her, Finn, and their triplets in the delivery room. Then each of her babies' tattoo pictures were lined up.

She stopped at the next set of photos—framed ones of Finn's parents and another of her mother and father. Arabella had no idea how he'd found the picture of her parents as it was from over a decade ago. But as she lightly traced the frame, she willed herself not to cry. It seemed that she now had all of her family, past and present, to display proudly on her giant family tree in the living room.

After a few beats, she forced herself to keep going and finally reached their bedroom door. It was closed with a large piece of paper taped to it, a black question mark filling the space.

Placing the unicorn down on the ground, she entered the room.

Finn lay on the bed, a kilt around his hips and nothing else.

She took a second to admire Finn's muscled chest and arms before reaching his face.

He grinned at her. "Like what you see, lass?"

"And here I expected you to have a rose clutched between your teeth."

"I've never given you a rose, so that would ruin the theme."

While she enjoyed bantering with her mate, Arabella smiled as she recalled each thing Finn had placed along the way. "I can't believe you remembered all of those little details."

He sat up. "Aye, of course I did. I remember anything related to you, love." He put out a hand. "Come. I have more surprises for you."

She did as he bid. "Let me guess? You naked and inside me?"

"In time." He brought her hand to his lips and kissed her skin. "First, I need to make sure you understand how much I want you, lass."

He maneuvered until he sat with his legs spread, and then he guided Arabella to stand between them. "Undress for me, love."

No sooner had she tugged her top off then Finn leaned forward and kissed her abdomen. The light flicks of his tongue sent heat straight between her thighs.

He chuckled, the vibrations only making her wetter.

His voice was husky as he said, "It's good to know that even after the trials of childbirth, you still want me, lass."

Running her fingers through his blond hair, she answered, "I'll always want you, Finn. Even if you grow a weird barb on your penis."

"I don't want to know where you got that idea."

She smiled. "I have quite the imagination."

"Do you now? Care to share some of that imagination with your mate?"

"Oh, I have lots to share. But later." She stepped back and finished undressing. The desire burning in Finn's eyes gave her the courage to do it as quickly as possible.

When she was done, she moved back between his legs and tossed up his kilt. Taking his hard cock in hand, she stroked a few times. "I want to have you inside me first. Then we can tease and play."

As she straddled Finn's thighs, his hands went to her hips. His eyes never moved from hers. "Take what you want from me, lass. I'm yours, always."

For a second, Arabella couldn't believe Finlay Stewart was her mate. But then her dragon spoke up. *Of course he is. He should be lucky to have us.*

Finn rubbed his thumbs against the skin of her hips and murmured, "Tell your dragon she can have me later. Right now, I'm yours, Arabella."

Raising her hips, she positioned Finn's cock at her entrance and slowly sank down. She was glad to be on a form of birth control, because she loved feeling his long, hard length as she took him in.

Once she had him to the hilt, she leaned forward and nipped his jaw. "Then take me, Finn, and show me how much you love me."

With a growl, Finn flipped them over and pressed one of her legs back. "After I'm done, you'll never doubt how much you mean to me."

Finn took her lips in a rough kiss. As he moved his hips and devoured her mouth, Arabella forgot about everything but her mate—the strong, wonderful male who made her laugh and treasured her as much as any dragonman could.

As she screamed his name, it also served as a reminder to

the world that Finn was her true mate, partner, and love of her life. No matter what happened in the future, they would have each other. And there was nothing they couldn't tackle together.

AUTHOR'S NOTE

Thanks for continuing Finn and Arabella's journey. I sense more for them in the future, but we'll see when that happens!

I know this book ended up being about all the MacKenzies, in addition to Finn and Arabella, but they're all tied together in a way. It also helped to tidy up quite a few dangling threads (Holly's pregnancy, Fergus and Gina's mate-claim frenzy) as well as to remind readers that Finn needed to both send a foster candidate to Stonefire and to allow someone from the Department of Dragon Affairs to come observe his clan. The person coming from the DDA will be the heroine of the next Lochguard book, *The Dragon's Discovery*. She's going to surprise Alistair Boyd in a quite a few ways. And because it's Alistair's book, you'll get to see more of his over-the-top mother and her crazy beaus. I'm still debating whether this book will come out in late 2018 or early 2019, but regardless the audio will be produced soon after it's released. (And while I can't always control my imagination, I sense Alistair's book will lead to one of two other stories: Chase McFarland and Dr. Layla MacFie's, or Cat MacAllister and Lachlan MacKinnon's. Both have been hinted at in previous books, so we'll see which ends up being book seven!)

Okay, with that out of the way I have some people I need to thank for helping me to get this book out to the world:

- To Becky Johnson and her team at Hot Tree Editing—you all are amazing. Becky gets me and helps my stories shine.
- To Clarissa Yeo of Yocla Designs—you yet again designed a beautiful cover that captures my couple and the hecticness of their family perfectly. I couldn't imagine my series without your magic.
- To Donna H., Alyson S., Iliana G., Sabrina D., and Sandy H.—My beta readers are amazing and provide valuable honesty. Not only that, they catch the little typos that slip through. All of you are appreciated more than you know. <3

And as always, I thank you, the reader, for supporting my dragons this long. When I first published *Healed by the Dragon* I had no idea that I'd be writing another story about Finn and Arabella three years later! Thanks a million times from my heart for not only reading, but for also spreading the word. Word-of-mouth is more powerful than you think.

My next release will be *The Forbidden* (Kelderan Runic Warriors #4), out in August 2018 in ebook format, with audio soon to follow.

Thanks so much for reading and I hope to see you at the end of the next book!

The Conquest
(Kelderan Runic Warriors #1)

Leader of a human colony planet, Taryn Demara has much more on her plate than maintaining peace or ensuring her people have enough to eat. Due to a virus that affects male embryos in the womb, there is a shortage of men. For decades, her people have enticed ships to their planet and tricked the men into staying. However, a ship hasn't been spotted in eight years. So when the blip finally shows on the radar, Taryn is determined to conquer the newcomers at any cost to ensure her people's survival.

Prince Kason tro de Vallen needs to find a suitable planet for his people to colonize. The Kelderans are running out of options despite the fact one is staring them in the face—Planet Jasvar. Because a group of Kelderan scientists disappeared there a decade ago never to return, his people dismiss the planet as cursed. But Kason doesn't believe in curses and takes on the mission to explore the planet to prove it. As his ship approaches Jasvar, a distress signal chimes in and Kason takes a group down to the planet's surface to explore. What he didn't expect was for a band of females to try and capture him.

As Taryn and Kason measure up and try to outsmart each other, they soon realize they've found their match. The only question is whether they ignore the spark between them and focus on their respective people's survival or can they find a path where they both succeed?

Excerpt:

Chapter One

Taryn Demara stared at the faint blip on the decades-old radar. Each pulse of light made her heart race faster. This is it. Her people might have a chance to survive.

Using every bit of restraint she had, Taryn prevented her voice from sounding too eager as she asked, "Are you sure it's a spaceship?"

Evaine Benoit, her head of technology, nodded. "Our equipment is outdated, but by the size and movement, it has to be a ship."

Taryn's heart beat double-time as she met her friend's nearly black-eyed gaze. "How long do we have before they reach us?"

"If they maintain their current trajectory, I predict eighteen hours, give or take. It's more than enough time to get the planet ready."

"Right," Taryn said as she stood tall again. "Keep me updated on any changes. If the ship changes course, boost the distress signal."

Evaine raised her brows. "Are you sure? The device is on its last legs. Any boost in power could cause a malfunction. I'm not sure my team or I can fix it again if that happens."

She gripped her friend's shoulder. "After eight years of waiting, I'm willing to risk it. I need that ship to reach Jasvar and send a team down to our planet."

Otherwise, we're doomed was left unsaid.

Without another word, Taryn raced out of the aging

technology command center and went in search of her best strategist. There was much to do and little time to do it.

Nodding at some of the other members of her settlement as she raced down the corridors carved into the mountainside, Taryn wondered what alien race was inside the ship on the radar. Over the past few hundred years, the various humanoid additions to the once human-only colony had added extra skin tones, from purple to blue to even a shimmery gold. Some races even had slight telepathic abilities that had been passed down to their offspring.

To be honest, Taryn didn't care what they looked like or what powers they possessed. As long as they were genetically compatible with her people, it meant Taryn and several other women might finally have a chance at a family. The "Jasvar Doom Virus" as they called it, killed off most male embryos in the womb, to the point only one male was born to every five females. Careful genealogical charts had been maintained to keep the gene pool healthy. However, few women were willing to share their partner with others, which meant the male population grew smaller by the year.

It didn't help that Jasvar had been set up as a low-technology colony, which meant they didn't have the tools necessary to perform the procedures in the old tales of women being impregnated without sex. The technique had been called in-something or other. Taryn couldn't remember the exact name from her great-grandmother's stories from her childhood.

Not that it was an option anyway. Jasvar's technology was a hodgepodge of original technology from the starter colonists and a few gadgets from their conquests and alien additions over the years. It was a miracle any of it still functioned.

The only way to prevent the extinction of her people was to capture and introduce alien males into their society.

Whoever had come up with the idea of luring aliens to the planet's surface and developing the tools necessary to get them to stay had been brilliant. Too bad his or her name had been lost to history.

Regardless of who had come up with the idea, Taryn was damned if she would be the leader to fail the Jasvarian colony. Since the old technology used to put out the distress signals was failing, Taryn had a different sort of plan for the latest alien visitors.

She also wanted their large spaceship and all of its technology.

Of course, her grand plans would be all for nothing if she couldn't entice and trap the latest aliens first. To do that, she needed to confer with Nova Drakven, her head strategist.

Rounding the last corner, Taryn waltzed into Nova's office. The woman's pale blue face met hers. Raising her silver brows, she asked, "Is it true about the ship?"

With a nod, Taryn moved to stand in front of Nova's desk. "Yes. It should be here in about eighteen hours."

Nova reached for a file on her desk. "Good. Then I'll present the plan to the players, and we can wait on standby until we know for sure where the visiting shuttle lands."

Taryn shook her head and started pacing. "I need you to come up with a new plan, Nova."

"Why? I've tweaked what went wrong last time. We shouldn't have any problems."

"It's not that." Taryn stopped pacing and met her friend's gaze. "This time, we need to do more than entice a few males to stay. Our planet was originally slated to be a low-tech colony, but with the problems that arose, that's no longer an option. We need supplies and knowledge, which means negotiating with the mother ship for their people."

"Let me get this straight—you want to convince the vastly technologically advanced aliens that we are superior, their crew's lives are in danger, and that they need to pay a ransom to get them back?"

Taryn grinned. "See, you do understand me."

Nova sighed. "You have always been crazy and a little reckless."

"Not reckless, Nova. Just forward-thinking. You stage the play, think of a few ideas about how to get the ship, and I'll find a way to make it work."

"Always the super leader to the rescue. Although one day, your luck may run out, Taryn."

Nova and Taryn were nearly the same age, both in their early thirties, and had grown up together. Nova was her best friend and one of the few people Taryn was unafraid to speak her fears with. "As long as my luck lasts through this ordeal, I'm okay with that. I can't just sit and watch our people despairing if another year or ten pass before there's new blood. If we had a way to get a message to Earth, it would make everything easier. But, we don't have that capability."

Nova raised her brows. "Finding a way to contact Earth or the Earth Colony Alliance might be an easier goal than taking over a ship."

"The message would take years to get there and who knows if the ECA would even send a rescue ship to such a distant colony." Taryn shook her head. "I can't rely on chance alone. I'll send a message from the alien ship, but I also want the technology to save us in the near future, too. I much prefer being in control."

Nova snorted. "Sometimes a little too much in control, in my opinion."

"A leader letting loose doesn't exactly instill confidence," she drawled.

"Then promise me that once you save the planet, you let

me show you some fun. No one should die before riding the sloping Veran waterfalls."

Taryn sighed and sank into the chair in front of Nova's desk. "Fine. But how about we focus on capturing the aliens first?"

Nova removed a sheaf of crude paper made from the purple wood of the local trees and took out an ink pot and golden feather. "I'll come up with a fool-proof capture plan, but I hope you keep me in the loop about what happens next."

"I will when it's time. I need to see who we're dealing with before making concrete plans."

Dipping her feather into the ink pot, Nova scratched a few notes on the purple paper. "Then let me get to work. The staging is mostly done already, but I need to think beyond that. Since we've never tried to capture a large ship before, it's going to take some time. I think someone captured a shuttle in the past, but we'll see if I can find the record."

"You always go on about how you love challenges."

"Don't remind me." She made a shooing motion toward the door. "And this is one of the few times I can tell my settlement leader to get lost and let me work."

Taryn stood. "If you need me, I'll be in the outside garden."

"Fine, fine. Just go. You're making it hard to concentrate." Nova looked up with a smile. "And you're also delaying my next project."

"Do I want to know?"

"It's called Operation Fun Times." Nova pointed her quill. "I sense you're going to land an alien this time. You're a talented individual, except when it comes to flirting. I'm going to help with that."

Shaking her head, Taryn muttered, "Have fun," and left her old-time friend to her own devices. Maybe someday

Nova would understand that while Taryn missed the antics of their youth, she enjoyed taking care of her people more.

Still, she'd admit that it would be nice to finally have the chance to get a man of her own. Most of her family was gone, and like many of the women of her age group, Taryn would love the option to start one.

Not now, Demara. You won't have a chance unless you succeed in capturing the visitors.

With the play planning in motion, Taryn had one more important task to set up before she could also pore through the records and look for ideas.

As much as she wished for everything to go smoothly, it could take a turn and end up horribly wrong. In that case, she needed an out. Namely, she needed to erase memories. The trick would be conferring with her head medicine woman to find the balance between erasing memories and rendering the aliens brain-dead. As the early Jasvarians had discovered, the forgetful plant was both a blessing and a curse. Without it, they'd never have survived this long. However, in the wrong dose, it could turn someone into a vegetable and ruin their chances.

Don't worry. Matilda knows what she's doing. Picking up her pace, Taryn exited the mountain into the late-day sun. The faint purple and blue hues of the mountains and trees were an everyday sight to her, but she still found the colors beautiful. Her great-grandmother's tales had been full of green leaves and blue skies back on Earth. A part of Taryn wanted to see another world, but the leader in her would never abandon the people of Jasvar.

Looking to the pinkish sky, she only hoped the visitors fell for her tricks. Otherwise, Taryn might have to admit defeat and prepare her people for the worst.

✲✲✲

Prince Kason tro el Vallen of the royal line of Vallen stared at his ship's main viewing screen. The blue, pink, and purple hues of the planet hid secrets Kason was determined to discover. After years of fighting his father's wishes and then the ensuing days of travel from Keldera to the unnamed planet, he was anxious to get started.

Aaric, his head pilot, stated, "Ten hours until we pull into orbit, your highness."

Kason disliked the title but had learned over time that to fight it was pointless. "Launch a probe to investigate."

"Yes, your highness."

As Aaric sent the request to the necessary staff, the silver-haired form of Ryven Xanna, Kason's best friend and the head warrior trainer on the ship, walked up to him. "We need to talk."

Kason nodded. Ryven would only ask to talk if it was important. "I can spare a few minutes. Aaric, you have the command."

The pair of them entered Kason's small office off the central command area. The instant the door slid shut, Ryven spoke up again. "Some of the men's markings are tinged yellow. They're nervous. No doubt thanks to the rumors of a monster on the planet's surface."

"There is no monster. There's a logical explanation as to why our team of scientists disappeared on Jasvar ten years ago."

"I agree with you, but logic doesn't always work with the lower-ranked officers and the common soldiers."

Kason clasped his hand behind his back. "You wouldn't ask to talk with me unless you have a solution. Tell me what it is, Ryv."

"I know it's not standard protocol for you to lead the first landing party, but if you go, it will instill courage in the others," Ryven answered.

Kason raised a dark-blue eyebrow. "Tell me you aren't among the nervous."

Ryven shrugged and pointed to one of the markings that peeked above his collar. "The dark blue color tells you all you need to know."

Dark blue signaled that a Kelderan was at peace and free of negative emotions.

"You are better at controlling your emotions than anyone I have ever met. You could be deathly afraid and would somehow keep your markings dark blue."

The corner of Ryven's mouth ticked up. "The trick has worked well for me over the years."

"We don't have time for reminiscing, Ryv. You're one of the few who speaks the truth to me. Don't change now."

"Honestly?" Ryven shrugged. "I'm not any more nervous or worried than any other mission. The unknown enemy just means we need to be cautious more than ever."

"Agreed. I will take the first landing party and leave Thorin in charge. Assemble your best warriors and send me a message when they're ready. I want to talk with them and instill bravery beforehand."

In a rare sign of emotion, Ryven gripped Kason's bicep. "Bravery is all well and fine, but if there is a monster we can't defeat, promise you'll pull back. Earning your father's praise isn't worth your life."

"I'm a little insulted at your implication. I wouldn't be a general in my own right if I lived by foolish displays of machismo."

Ryven studied him a second before adding, "Just because you're a general now doesn't mean you have to talk like one with me."

Kason remembered their childhood days, before they'd

both been put on the path of a warrior. Kason and Ryven had pulled pranks on their siblings and had reveled in coming up with stupid competitions, such as who could reach the top of a rock face first in freezing temperatures or who could capture a poisonous shimmer fly with nothing but their fingers.

But neither of them were boys anymore. Displaying emotion changed the color of the rune-like markings on their bodies, which exposed weakness. Warriors couldn't afford to show any weakness. It was one of the reasons higher-ranked officers weren't allowed to take wives, not even if they found one of their potential destined brides; the females would become easy targets.

Not that Kason cared. A wife would do nothing to prove his worth as a soldier to his father, the king. On top of that, being a warrior was all Kason knew. Giving it up would take away his purpose.

Pushing aside thoughts of his father and his future, Kason motioned toward the door. "Go and select the best soldiers to assist with the landing party. I have my own preparations to see to."

"I'll go if you promise one thing."

"What?"

"You allow me to be part of the landing party."

Kason shook his head. "I can't. In the event of my death, I need you here."

"Thorin is your second and will assume command. Give me the honor of protecting you and the others during the mission."

Deep down, in the place where Kason locked up any emotion, a small flicker of indecision flashed. Ryven was more Kason's brother than his real-life brother, Keltor.

Yet to contain Ryven on the ship would be like a slap in the face; the honor of protecting a prince such as Kason was the highest form of trust to one of the Kelderan people.

Locking down his emotions, Kason followed his logical brain. "You may attend. But on-planet, you become a soldier. I can't treat you as my friend."

Ryven put out a hand and Kason shook it to seal their agreement. "I'm aware of protocol. I teach it day in and day out. But I will be the best damned soldier of the group. And if it comes to it, I will push you out of the way to protect your life."

Kason released his friend's hand. "I won't let it come to that."

"Good. When shall we rendezvous?"

Glancing at the small screen projecting an image of the multicolored planet, he answered, "Nine hours. That will give all of us a chance to sleep before performing the pre-battle ritual. You can lead the men through their meditation and warm-up maneuvers after that."

Ryven nodded. "I'll see you then."

The trainer exited the room, and Kason turned toward his private viewing screen to study the planet rumored to host the most feared monster in the region. One that had supposedly taken hundreds of men's lives over the years. The story was always the same—a small contingent of men disappeared from any group that landed on the surface. No one remembered how they were captured or if they were even alive. Anytime a second party landed, a few more would be taken.

Over time, the planet had earned a reputation. Even the most adventure-seeking ruffians had stayed away.

However, Kason dismissed it as folklore. Whatever was on that planet, he wouldn't allow it to defeat him or his men. Kason would bring honor to his family with a victory. He also hoped to give his people the gift of a new planet. Keldera was overpopulated, and its resources were stretched beyond the limit. The Kelderans desperately needed a new colony and hadn't been able to locate one that was suitable. The planet on the view screen showed all the signs of being a near-perfect fit.

Even if the fiercest monster in existence resided on that planet, Kason wouldn't retreat from an enemy. Death was an accepted part of being a Kelderan soldier.

————————————

The Conquest is now available in paperback. Learn more at: www.jessiedonovan.com

ABOUT THE AUTHOR

Jessie Donovan has sold over half a million books, has given away hundreds of thousands more to readers for free, and has even hit the *NY Times* and *USA Today* best-seller lists. She is best known for her dragon-shifter series, but also writes about magic users, aliens, and even has an upcoming crazy romantic comedy set in Scotland. When not reading a book, attempting to tame her yard, or traipsing around some foreign country on a shoestring, she can often be found interacting with her readers on Facebook. Check out her page: www.facebook.com/JessieDonovanAuthor

And don't forget to sign-up for her newsletter to receive sneak peeks and inside information. You can sign-up for her newsletter at: www.jessiedonovan.com

Made in the USA
Columbia, SC
25 May 2020